A Twisted Mission
An Olympia Brown Mystery

by

Judith Campbell

Mainly Murder Press, LLC
PO Box 290586
Wethersfield, CT 06129-0586
www.mainlymurderpress.com

Mainly Murder Press

Editor: Judith K. Ivie
Cover Designer: Karen A. Phillips
Cover photo by Judith Campbell

All rights reserved

Names, characters and incidents depicted in this book are products of the author's imagination or are used fictitiously. Any resemblance to actual events, organizations, or persons, living or dead, is entirely coincidental and beyond the intent of the author or the publisher.

No part of this book may be reproduced or transmitted in any form or by any means, electronic or mechanical, including photocopying, recording, or by any information storage and retrieval system, without permission in writing from the publisher.

Copyright © 2015 by Judith Campbell
Paperback ISBN 978-0-9861780-0-9

Published in the United States of America by

Mainly Murder Press, LLC
PO Box 290586
Wethersfield, CT 06129-0586
www.MainlyMurderPress.com

*Dedicated to my LGBT friends--
you know who you are.*

Over my straight life I have had many LGBT friends who have enriched my life, offered a shoulder to cry on or, when one was needed, accepted my offer of one. I have married and buried some of you and christened/blessed your children. I've been a straight ally and advocate for LGBT rights and issues most of my adult life and will continue to be so, because we ain't done yet!

Many of my LGBT characters, especially Father Jim, are composites of beloved and respected LGBT and LGBTQ friends. Thank you for all you have given me. I offer up these stories and characters as an outward and visible sign of the inner and spiritual grace that only true friendship can give. It is all of our responsibility to continue the work of bringing understanding, compassion and acceptance to a still reluctant world.

~

Acknowledgments

Thank you to my husband, Chris Stokes, professional Englishman and alpha reader; my son Colin, who is my go-to wine and sports expert; The 3 on 3 Writers in Kingston: Pam, Vaughn, Ruthy, Charlotte, Robert, Jon, Melody, Florence, Jacquie, Fran, Dolores and Johanna. You have hearts of gold, ears of steel and honest words, thank you. Thanks also to the OBL writers, who have a life tenancy in my heart; to Pamela Kelley, sister author of mysteries and romances and next door neighbor from heaven; and finally to Simon and Katie, two fabulous felines who interfere with almost everything I do, and I wouldn't have it any other way.

Praise for the Olympia Brown Mysteries

"In *A Predatory Mission,* author and minister, the Reverend Dr. Judith Campbell takes on the highly charged subject of clergy sex abuse. She writes honestly and clearly about this much talked about but poorly understood subject. She does not back away from the truth or the untoward and illustrates plainly how a predator sexually assaults those whom he was called to pastor. I have added Campbell's book as required reading, next to those of Nathaniel Hawthorne, John Updike and Sinclair Lewis, in the courses and programs I offer on clergy sexual misconduct. Like Hawthorne in *The Scarlet Letter,* Campbell writes about the real and serious damage done to people by clergy hypocrisy and abuse of power. But unlike Hawthorne, her novel is accessible and entertaining. You will not be able to put it down."
    The Reverend Dr. Deborah J. Pope-Lance, minister, psychotherapist and consultant on clergy malpractice and creating safe congregations

"*An Unspeakable Mission* is an engaging and thought-provoking story of two dedicated and impassioned clerics struggling to find the truth when secrets and silence are the expected norms. And when 21st century religion gets involved with religious and cultural expectations of the past, the story doesn't always turn out as expected. I kept turning the pages to see what would happen next."
    Rev. Keith Kron, Director of the Transitions Office for the Unitarian Universalist Association

"Judith Campbell does a superb job in the follow-up to her suspense/thriller, *A Deadly Mission,* as Olympia Brown is once again tangled up in the personal life of one of her students, an ugly secret too horrible to speak of, and a death that looks suspiciously like murder!"
Brenda Scott, Manchester Contemporary Literary Examiner, Examiner.com

"Rev. Judith Campbell has done it again in *An Unspeakable Mission,* her second in the Olympia Brown mystery series. Using her experience as an ordained minister as well as a writer, Judith deftly weaves a compelling mystery about the death of an abusive alcoholic in a suspicious house fire, with the horrific subjects of incest and domestic violence. …a perfect balance between building suspense and giving voice to victims who can't speak for themselves, proving in the process that what often seems obvious ... isn't."
Dawn Braash, avid reader and owner of Bunch of Grapes, the flagship bookstore of Martha's Vineyard where authors and readers find everything they are looking for.

The Olympia Brown "Mission Mystery" Series
(in order of publication)

A Deadly Mission
An Unspeakable Mission
A Despicable Mission
An Unholy Mission
A Predatory Mission
An Improper English Mission
A Singular Mission
A Twisted Mission (The Prequel)

Author's Note

A Twisted Mission is set in the early 1990s, before computers and cell phones took over the world. Hence, Olympia uses land lines and does not own a computer, so when she decides to add a little spice to her social life, she starts reading the personals in paper-and-ink newspapers. (Remember those?) rather than joining an electronic dating service or checking a potential someone out on Facebook.

The experience of writing a book is as much of an adventure for me as I hope reading it will be for you. My mysteries (psych-thrillers, actually, a subset of the larger mystery/thriller genre) usually focus on ethical, moral or social dilemmas. Protagonist Olympia Brown finds herself compelled to get involved and do what she can to make things right, often at her own peril. Otherwise, it wouldn't be a thriller, would it? Technically they are cozies, meaning they are not graphically violent or erotically explicit, and the action takes place over a relatively short period of time. When sex and violence do occur (I do, after all, write about human behavior.), I usually move them away from center stage.

My books seem to be enjoyed in equal numbers by men and women. The most common comment is, "I can't put the thing down," followed by, "When's the next one coming out? I'll take it!" You can find lots of great reviews on my website and on Amazon.

A Twisted Mission is a direct response to so many of you writing to me and asking to know more about Olympia's back story. It is by popular request a "prequel" to the Mission Mysteries featuring The Reverend Doctor, and one-time Professor, Olympia Brown. The first in the series used to be *A Deadly Mission*. Now it is *A Twisted Mission,* but as with the others, each story stands on its own. You can read them in sequence or skip around. My readers seem to do both.

The theme of bullying is a very timely one. I don't think there is a one of us who has not been bullied directly or witnessed it. It's getting a lot of media attention right now, and that is a good thing, but the attention has not stopped it from happening. Bullies need to be called out and exposed, and we all know this is easier said than done. In this book I try and talk about the bully with as much eventual compassion as I do his victim. The truth is, bullies often get that way because they themselves were victims of a bully. The underlying message in the book is to speak up. Get help. Find an advocate.

The second theme in this particular story, and one that runs throughout many of my books, is lesbian, gay, bisexual, transgender (LGBT) issues. In the early 1990s these issues were much more difficult to speak of and deal with. There is no doubt that in the US, at least, and many western European countries, life for the LGBT community is much safer but not completely so. LGBT people are an ongoing part of my stories because they are an ongoing part of all of our lives, whether or not we are fully aware of it. It's just one more way of being human, and we need more understanding of that.

By way of introducing you to this book and the whole series, I think the easiest thing to do will be to answer the Frequently Asked Questions (FAQs) that I almost always get when I do a book talk. They are also sent to me through my website at www.judithcampbell-holymysteries.com or posted on my Facebook pages, Judith Campbell and Judith Campbell Author. These appear in the Meet the Author section at the end of this book.

Judith Campbell

One

Without warning the snake slashed and zigzagged across the path just inches from his feet. He'd almost stepped on it. Now, frozen in place with his heart pounding, sweating profusely, he watched as the moving grasses off to his right indicated the direction of the reptile's speedy escape. Then he looked around to see if anyone had witnessed the incident but saw no one. He was morbidly afraid of snakes and had been since the day his father, drunk and trying to make a man of him, threw one in his face and then laughed when he screamed, fell on the ground and wet himself. The only thing he feared more than snakes these days was someone finding out about it. This was a close call, but so far his luck was holding. No one saw it. When his breathing and heart rate returned to normal, he continued along the path toward the crew shack, stamping his feet, waving his arms and making as much noise and commotion as he could.

Two

Across the street and up the short hill from the camp ground, a painfully thin and desperately unhappy young man scribbled a few words on a scrap of paper, folded it and pushed it deep into his jeans pocket. Then he climbed up on top of the battered old wooden dresser next to his bed. Careful to keep his balance, he tossed one end of a twisted sheet up and over the ceiling beam directly above him. He knotted it, yanked on it to test its strength and then secured it. Once that was done, he tied the other end around his neck. He had taken great care with the measurements so that when jumped off and kicked the shoddy dresser away from beneath him, his feet would not reach the floor. He hoped, even dared to pray, it would be quick.

Three

A fiftieth birthday, whatever else it might be, is a milestone. It can be a warning signal, a turning point or both. It can be loudly celebrated or quietly ignored, but it cannot be denied. It is a time when many will choose to step back and take stock. The Rev. Dr. Olympia Brown had just reached that significant event with as many questions in her mind as she had years logged on the calendar. The two at the very top of the list were, should she continue as a college chaplain and professor of humanities and religion at Merriwether College, or should she leave academia and take on a full time parish ministry?

On the nonprofessional and more personal front there were more questions. Now that her two sons, Malcolm and Randall, were technically out of the safe suburban nest, her status as a not-very-swinging single was lonely. Maybe she should be more proactive about creating a little more action in that corner of her life. Maybe she should move out of her white, middle class, three-bedroom expanded Cape in the town with the good schools and buy a condo in Boston or Cambridge. That would certainly ease her commute and save money on gas.

She could take her mother's advice, let nature take its course and wait for the universe to reveal what the future might offer—but Olympia rarely took her mother's advice, so she eliminated that one even before she wrote it down. And so it was on a spectacular summer day in early June, she was sitting in her back yard, sipping iced tea and making a list …

or maybe it was a five-year plan. Olympia hadn't decided which. In big block letters she created three columns across the top of the sheet of paper: Done, Yet to Be Done, and Wildest Dreams/Extreme Bucket List.

If nothing else, and there was a whole lot of else, Olympia Brown was methodical and well organized. She typically set reasonable goals for herself and then in her own determined fashion strategized how to reach them. At age fifty, she knew who she was and pretty much what she wanted out of life. She also knew what she was and was not prepared give up in order to bring that about, or so she thought.

However, nothing that was about to happen in the coming summer was on this list and no one, not even the practical plotter could have predicted or planned for what did happen. She couldn't possibly know it, but it seemed she was at the mercy of a host of gods and goddesses who were bored and decided to have a bit of fun. The object of their ungodly mischief of fancy and foolishness was a middle-aged, slightly restless college professor who in one unguarded moment said she might be ready for a change.

Olympia's mother also told her, "Be careful what you wish for." It would have been good advice, had she listened, but she didn't, and therein hangs the tale.

There was no doubt she was restless. Her present academic rut was sweet and secure and far too comfortable, but it paid the bills. On the list of things she might possibly do to brighten up her life were: lie about her age and weight and join a dating service, take a trip, change jobs, get another cat, write the great American novel, or simply get away from it all and go camping for a couple of weeks.

Being a college professor gave her the unique advantage of having almost three months every summer to herself, which were intended to be spent in professional study and research. When her boys were younger this allowed her to be home and keep an eagle eye on them as they stumbled through their teenage ups and downs. Now, with the two of them pretty much on their own, it was far too quiet in her empty nest, particularly at night.

She looked down at her possibilities list and wondered what else she might add to it. The words "go camping" caught her eye, and she knew she had her answer. Not two days earlier she'd received a call from Brad Davies, the managing director of Orchards Cove, a religious campground and conference center in southern Maine, asking if she'd consider being their summer chaplain. If she accepted, he said she would be responsible for Sunday morning services, as well as short daily morning and evening gatherings for meditation and prayer, and she was to be available for pastoral care if needed. Other than this, her time would be her own. He was doing his level best to make it sound appealing.

That's what they always say, she thought, twirling a pencil in her fingers, but what the heck, the timing couldn't be better, and the price was right. While they would not offer her much in salary, she would have all meals and her pick of a prime spot in the campground. There she could commune with the creatures and beasties that go bump in the night. She'd have a chance to get back in touch with the sounds and smells of nature, maybe write a little poetry, if she so desired, and think about what she might do for the second and shorter phase of her life.

Yes, she nodded in agreement with herself. A summer alone in a tent was the perfect solution. It would offer time to think, no doubt about that, and she would have some interesting and diverse people with whom she could discuss her options, if she wished. Then there was the purely social side of it. The possibilities were multiple and well worth investigating. Any number of single men she knew, both gay and straight, thought of the place as a happy hunting ground. That did it. Olympia smiled at her good fortune. She went back into the house and picked up the handset of the new portable phone she'd just purchased and started to tap in the number she'd written on the wall beside the sink.

"Hi, Brad? It's Olympia Brown. You called me a couple of days ago asking if I wanted to be the summer chaplain up there. Well, I've thought about it, and the answer is yes. What do I need to know, and when should I arrive?"

"That is terrific, Olympia. I was hoping you'd do it. I'll send out everything you need to know, including a map of the campground, this afternoon. You'll need to be up here by June 20th for our staff and leadership orientation weekend. The official season doesn't begin for another week after that, but there's always more to do than we anticipate, so we try and give ourselves the time. Then if we get lucky, we can take it easy for the last few days before the merry madness begins."

Olympia looked at the Audubon calendar hanging on the kitchen wall. Departure date was less than a week away. "Anything I should know or be aware of before I actually get in the car?"

Brad paused for a nanosecond before responding. "Well, yes, no or maybe. I'll tell you and then let you decide for yourself. We have a new crew boss this year. He's come up through the ranks, starting as a camper. Then he was a dishwasher, and then he went onto the maintenance crew. He was the logical choice, but, well, let's just say he can be a little demanding. He's had some scuffles along the way. He can be a bit of a perfectionist. So while we need to get the work done around here, we want the crew to be happy and have a good time while they are doing it. Do you see what I mean?"

"I think so. Tell me more," said Olympia.

"His name is Derek Jamison. He's definitely earned his stripes in terms of hands-on experience, and he has every qualification to do a good job, plus he's got the life-long history of coming here to go along with it. That counts for a lot at Orchards Cove. It's my job as manager to keep an eye on him, but since you'll be doing the religious and spiritual component of the orientation program, I'd like you to cast a casual eye in his direction and tell me what you think. Then, if it seems necessary, we do what needs to be done to guide and support him."

"Or let him go," said Olympia.

"Oh, I don't think it will come anywhere near being that serious. He means well, he just bears watching. Who knows, he might have totally gotten past all of it with a third year of college under his belt. I just thought I'd give you a little heads up."

"College can work wonders with bringing on maturity. It's what I do during the year. I help young women grow up in spite of themselves." And I'm good and sick of it, she thought. I really do need a summer away from everything familiar, and it's been dropped right into my lap. I didn't even have to ask. This is looking better and better.

"OK, Brad, send me the stuff, and I'll go dig around in the attic and the cellar and see what the mice have left of my camping equipment."

She hung up with the sound of his pleasant chuckle bubbling in her ear. Brad was a good man. She'd worked with him before on events and special projects in the local district, and she knew him to be a person she could trust. She smiled and ruffled her fingers through her short salt and pepper hair, then stretched her arms high above her head and arched her back, trying not to hear the creaks and cracks the movement produced. It was going to be a good summer, just what the doctor—in this case, the Reverend Doctor—ordered. In September, she'd go back to Merriwether and either sign another contract or write a letter of resignation effective the following June. Only time would tell which it would be. Who knows, she thought with a sly smile, there might even be an option waiting for me out there I haven't even met yet, preferably an option of the opposite sex.

The one remaining thing she needed to do before she started packing was call her best friend, Father Jim Sawicki. He was a Roman Catholic priest and her closest collegial confidante. The two were as different as chalk and cheese. He was well ordered, neat and conservative in dress and manner, and she ... was not. But despite, or maybe because of, their differences, the two had a bond of friendship and trust that transcended religious denomination. Any time Olympia had to make a big decision, she discussed it first with Jim. They'd met when they both were part of a doctoral study group at Harvard Divinity School some years back. Since then their careers had run pretty much parallel to one another. Jim was a Professor of Theology and World Religions at Allston College, just west of Boston. He was also the associate parish priest at St. Bartholomew's Parish in Dorchester. She was a professor of Humanities and Religion at Merriwether College, a women's institution that was only a couple of blocks north of the Harvard Divinity School in Cambridge, Massachusetts.

Their job proximity and shared interests allowed for frequent lunch and coffee dates in and around Harvard Square. If they were feeling expansive, and time permitted, they would sneak away for an entire afternoon to an art gallery or one of the local museums and call it scholarly research. Olympia reached for the phone and dialed his number. When he didn't answer, she left a short message along with her own number and asked him to call her at home.

Four

On the following Friday morning, Olympia wedged the oversized pet carrier, with two murderous cats glaring out at her, into the last remaining space in her beloved vintage blue Volkswagen microbus. To say she was loaded for bear would be an understatement. She was loaded for a dozen bears.

Olympia Brown liked to be prepared for all eventualities, and judging from the contents of the van, she was. This was going to be a long overdue vacation and adventure. She caught a quick glimpse of herself in the rearview mirror and smiled her approval. She was sporting a fresh-clipped, no maintenance haircut and wearing her best loose and comfy driving clothes: a soft, well-worn tee shirt, Capri length slacks that covered her middle-aged knees and sturdy, buckle-on sandals.

In the tightly packed suitcase, along with everything else, was a new bathing suit. It was a slimming crisscross style designed to minimize middle-aged middles, but maybe that was expecting too much of any garment. She shrugged. What the hell, she thought, quoting Popeye, I yam what I yam. South coastal Maine, here I come.

As she rattled along Route 95 North she was trying to listen to NPR over the signature tinny rattle of a Volkswagen engine, but it was fast becoming a lost cause. The signal was fading in and out so erratically that she finally gave up, turned off the radio and let her mind wander where it might. She started with mentally going over the packing list. She had treated herself to a brand new, lightweight, easy to pitch tent with an attached screen house, no less, and an even more self-indulgent free-standing, electric blue dining canopy. Her old Coleman camp stove still worked, and she remembered exactly how to light the white-fuel pump-up mantle lantern, a survival skill requiring delicacy, dexterity, a lot of patience and, on occasion, a few well-aimed curses.

She had adequate rain gear, a new folding cot, air mattress and sleeping bag, cat food and an emergency litter box, unsexy but warm flannel pajamas and a sturdy flashlight for middle-of-the-night trips to the bathroom. A plastic tub with a snap-on lid contained basic kitchen supplies and would later double as a raccoon-proof dry food storage bin.

She could have continued reviewing the mental inventory for another several miles, but her mind drifted back to her conversation with Brad Davies and the possibly troublesome crew boss. Brad had been deliberately vague about the details of his concern, so she was left with an enormous question mark which vanished as she turned left off the main road into the Orchards Cove Campground (members only) and pulled to a stop in front of a faded split rail fence. She had no sooner turned off the engine than she looked into the side-view mirror and saw a broadly smiling young man wearing faded jeans and a blue and white crew shirt trotting toward her. He slowed to a stop beside her open window and held out his hand.

"Reverend Olympia Brown, driving a well-used VW van, will be looking for a camping space? We've been expecting you. I'm Derek Jamison. I'm the crew boss up here, and I've been assigned to work the campground today. I'm the official meeter and greeter and assigner of spaces. I've got a nice one all ready for you. It's right on the big circle near the washhouse. You'll be able to get to everything."

Hmmm, thought Olympia. That is exactly what I don't want. She smiled through the open window and continued holding his strong smooth hand. Firmly.

"Why, thank you, Derek. That's really kind of you. Efficient, too. However, Brad Davies told me I could have my pick of spots. I was thinking of something farther out in the woods."

He was undeterred. "That's a long walk to the washroom, Reverend, and you'll get lots more little critters stealing your food and starting skunk fights under your picnic table." He didn't mention age, but his eyes and slightly patronizing manner said it for him.

She smiled and patted his hand. "I'm sure you have my best interests in mind, Derek, but I do have my heart set on being on the outermost edge and not in the middle. I've camped alone in the woods for more years than you've had hot breakfasts, and I get along just fine with skunks and raccoons. We usually come to an understanding by the end of the second day. So lead on, if you will. My mind's made up."

The gentle humor was lost on him. "Well, if you insist. Just wait here, and I'll get you a map."

If there was one, Olympia chose to ignore the slight chill in his voice. "No need. I already have one. I'd like site C-11, if it's available."

He looked dismayed. "But that's the last one on the path. It's seriously out there, Ma'am. You'll be really isolated."

"That's the plan, at least for now anyway. I promise I'll move in closer if I feel the need, and if that happens I'll even let you say I told you so, but that's where I'm going today."

This, too, was lost on Derek as he waved her on with a perfunctory, "Just holler if you need anything, OK?"

He means well, she told herself as she negotiated the tree roots and the dips along the path that led to her outpost. She was familiar with the personality type. She'd had a few of them in her classes at Merriwether College. Once they got an idea of how things ought to be, factual evidence be damned, it took everything short of an act of Congress to get them to change their minds. It was usually easier to go around them than to push back unless, of course, they got so focused they were a danger to themselves or another person. Derek Jamison is new at the job, and he's trying to get it right, she told herself. He'll be OK once he gets used to things.

Olympia backed the van onto the campsite, disembarked and shook the kinks out of her back and her behind. She looked at the jumble in the van and thought, where the hell do I start? First things first; the cats. They could not be allowed to run free until she was sure they were used to where they were. She pushed a handful of dry food through the grating on the top of their carrier, and while they were busy scrabbling for it, she opened the door and shoved in a dish of water and the traveling litter box. Now she could really begin.

It had been a while since Olympia had set up a tent, but she was damned if she'd ask for help. She would do it by herself, come hell or high water. Start by reading the directions, Olympia. Tents have changed in the last twenty years.

In the process every one of her fifty years reminded her she was not only out of practice, but she was far too easily running out of breath. Nonetheless she soldiered on. Before long she was hammering down the final stake with a handy rock and surveying her handiwork. The tent was up. The sides and top were taut, the zippers all worked, and the folding camp bed she set up inside did not collapse or fold up on her when she stretched out on it. Best of all, the attached screen house easily accommodated the two aluminum folding chairs and plastic coffee table she'd stuffed into the van at the last minute. While she hadn't thought of it until that very minute, it was also a perfect cat enclosure. The dining canopy was less trouble to put up and perfectly covered the picnic table so that she could stand and cook and eat and even entertain guests out of the rain. At least that's what it said on the box it came in. Time and a good rainstorm would tell.

"Not bad," said a male voice from behind her.

Olympia leapt up and turned around in one startled motion. It was Derek. She'd not heard him approach. He was smiling.

"I guess you do know your way around a campsite in the woods. That was real quick, Ma'am. Private enough for you out here?" He smiled and looked around.

"It's perfect, thank you. Sorry for the startle response, I didn't hear you coming."

"That's OK. I've learned how to move quietly when I want to. I don't like to disturb the little creatures out here." He squatted down beside the cat carrier, poked his finger through the mesh and began stroking the first available furry face. "These your cats?"

Olympia beamed with the love and pride of ownership. "They are indeed. The big orange tabby is Thunderfoot, and the little tortoiseshell is Whitefoot. They won't be any trouble. I've camped with them before."

"They're cute, but I guess I'm more of a dog person. Dogs do what you tell them. Cats do what they want."

And there's something wrong with that, thought Olympia.

"Each to his own," she said and then added, "Can you show me where the electrical hook-up is? The map said each campsite has water and electric."

He pointed to a post beside a towering pine tree. "The faucet's over there, cold water only. If you want hot water, you'll have to heat it or carry it from the wash house. I'm afraid the electric isn't all the way out here yet. I'll tell the crew to get on it. We didn't think we'd need it so soon."

"I can wait," she said with a forced brightness. "I've gone whole summers without electricity. There's no rush."

"I'll do what I can, Ma'am. You take care now."

Derek Jamison turned on his heel and started back down the path. He was swinging his arms and whistling now, and Olympia wondered what that was all about.

She watched him padding down the path back toward the office shed where he would meet and greet and settle in the last of the seasonal staff. While a few of them shared or had private staff cottages, one or two, like Olympia, would choose the quieter and more contemplative option, a tent at the edge of the woods with the skunks and the raccoons—and who knows what else. Thoughts of Henry David Thoreau completed the idyllic image in her mind. This was just what she needed, a place of her own far from the madding crowd and time to think.

Five

Olympia heard the clanging of the dinner bell and checked her watch. It was 5:25. Crew and staff supper was scheduled for 5:30. Dinner for the conferees would be served at 6:30, once the season was officially opened, and then she would be expected to eat with them. But tonight it was everyone to the table and then on to the first full staff and crew orientation in the Big Hall. There she and other staff would be introduced to the crew, and they all would meet and mingle with this year's board of trustees at a make-your-own-sundae party.

Orientations were a necessary part of any start-up, and she would respectfully do what was expected of her; but after that, and in the presence of all you can eat ice cream and toppings, all bets were off. It was every woman for herself, and she would be first in line. Olympia had a remarkable fondness for ice cream, right up there with molasses raisin cookies and white wine and hot fresh coffee. There was more, but it had been too long a time since she'd indulged in that particular activity, sigh. For now it would have to be ice cream.

Before setting off she wet her hands under the outdoor faucet, splashed water on her face and neck and then, using the last drops, smoothed her flyaway hair into place. After checking the cats for food and water and making sure their wire cage was secure, Olympia was ready to meet and greet. More than that, she was ready to eat. Putting up a tent was hungry work, and Olympia was famished.

She joined the slow trickle of people moving up the road toward the dining hall, affectionately named The Quagmire or Quag, for short. Once inside she looked around. The only person in the room she recognized was Derek Jamison. He was sitting at a full table on the far side of the room, surrounded by tanned and healthy looking young men and women. They were all wearing the signature Orchards Cove blue and white crew tee-shirts. Olympia spotted a table with a few empty chairs, so she walked over and sat down next to a pleasant looking woman dressed all in white. Without waiting to be asked, she introduced herself and learned the names of the camp nurse, Ellie Chapman; the Office Manager, Ruthy Blake; the assistant cook, Joan Barrow; and her husband, Dan Barrow, who was the camp musician and after-dinner song leader. He was called Dan Dan the Music Man by one and all. Olympia hated camp-singing after meals, but she graciously didn't say that to Dan. She was paid staff, she was a team player and, like it or not, she'd sing.

This could be a long summer, was her first thought, but she wasn't allowed to take it any further. Just as the serving bowls of salad were being carried to the tables, Brad Davies burst into the room, and the howl of an approaching ambulance shattered the air outside the building. He waved his arms over his head and called for silence.

"Olympia, Ellie, we've got an emergency in the crew dorm. One of the new guys, Spider MacCormack, has had a bad accident. You two come with me. I want the rest of you to stay here. My assistant, Katie Simon, will be in charge. I'll come back and tell you everything as soon as I can, but for now, please stay here. The last thing we need is people getting in the way of the paramedics."

While the rest of the staff and crew members erupted into shocked and anxious questions of who and what had happened, Olympia and Ellie stood as one and raced across the dining room. Once outside on the wooden porch they set off across the street toward the crew dorm, where they could see flashing lights and hear the shouts of emergency crew.

"What happened? How bad is it?"

"Shouldn't we go in and help?"

Brad shook his head and held up his hand. "It's bad. I think it's probably best we stay outside and wait until they call us. These people know their business, and I don't want us to be in the way."

"What happened?" asked Ellie.

"Talk about coincidence. I just happened to be walking by the dorm on the way over here and heard a crash. I ran in there and found Spider hanging from a ceiling beam in his bunkroom. I think I got there in time, at least I hope I did. I know he was breathing, gagging really, when I got him down. I called 911 from the pay phone in the common room. Thank God we decided to put one in there, and double thank God I always carry a Swiss Army knife. It may have saved his life."

"Oh, nooo!" wailed Olympia.

Ellie Chapman bit into her knuckle and shook her head.

It wasn't long before Olympia could see the uniformed men coming out of the crew shack. They were pushing a gurney holding the blanket-swathed young person with an oxygen mask clamped on his chalk white face. Wide yellow strapping kept everything in place. Even from where they stood, it was clear to them he was in bad shape but still alive.

Brad put his hand on Olympia's shoulder. "If you don't mind, I'd like you to ride with him to the hospital. If he needs last rites, or whatever we do in that situation, then do it. If he doesn't, then pray your heart out that he won't be permanently brain damaged. I have no idea if, or for how long, he'd been without enough oxygen." Brad choked back what might have been a sob and turned to Ellie.

"They've got enough medical people in the ambulance. I need you to help me decide what to tell everyone. You OK with that?"

Ellie, ashen faced, gulped and nodded. "Sure, Brad."

When the ambulance pulled away, siren screeching and lights flashing, Brad and Ellie sat down hip-to-hip on the wooden steps of the crew shack front porch. They were almost in shock. Finally, Brad reached into his pocket for a handkerchief, wiped his forehead and the back of his neck and then his eyes.

"What the hell do I do now? What do I tell them in the dining hall?"

Ellie wiggled around so she was facing him. "I suggest you tell them as much of the truth as you can, just not all of it. I say that because we don't yet know all of it. We say that Spider MacCormack had a freak accident and is seriously injured. Tell them that you found him in time and called 911, and we don't yet know the full extent of his injuries. Assure them he is on the way to the hospital, and Olympia, the Summer Chaplain, has gone along with him in the ambulance. She'll call as soon as there is anything to report. But first you need to call his parents and tell them the same thing you are going to tell the people in the dining room. Right now, I don't think you need to tell them that his injuries may have been self-inflicted."

"Jesus Christ!" said Brad Davies.

"Do you want me to call them? I've probably had more experience than you have with this sort of thing. It never gets any easier, but at least I've done it before."

"No, Ellie, I think that would be a cop-out. This kind of thing isn't in the job description, but it comes with the territory. I'm the Camp Director, and I need to do it. Just stay there with me when I do, OK?"

"What do you know about him, Brad? Did he seem troubled? Were there any warning signs that you picked up?"

"Not really. He was quiet. He was tall and skinny, really skinny, and kind of awkward. He was no sportsman, and come to think of it, I never saw him on the beach. I knew he was shy, but I thought a summer up here would help him with some of that. That's one of the reasons I hired him. Who knows, it may be partly why he applied for the job."

"People can be really cruel, you know, even here at Orchards Cove. Did you ever catch anyone picking on him or making fun of him?" asked Ellie.

Brad shook his head. "Not that I really noticed, but then, they wouldn't do it in front of me, would they?"

"Not likely." She stood up and stretched and then brushed the sand and dust off the back of her white shorts. "Come on, let's get the worst part over first. We'll call his parents. Then they can be in direct contact with the hospital. Where's he from?"

"Not far. Portsmouth, New Hampshire. They can be at Maine Medical in less than two hours."

"Welcome to beautiful, peaceful Orchards Cove, where a stranger is only a friend you haven't met yet," said Ellie.

"Damn damn damn," said Brad. He was alternately clenching and flexing his fingers.

"Let's just hope to God he makes it," said Ellie.

"Don't even go there," said Brad.

Inside the ambulance the medics were doing everything they had been trained to do. Their job was to save lives, and they were working flat out to save this one. Seated in the passenger seat next to the driver, Olympia was alternately holding her breath and taking in great gulps of antiseptic smelling air while praying as she'd never prayed before in her life. Spider, strapped to the gurney with the paramedic monitoring every breath, looked like a broken doll, a broken boy doll.

When Brad and Ellie returned to the dining hall, the room fell completely silent. It had been less than an hour since Brad had made the announcement, but it seemed to him like half a lifetime. He cleared his throat. He didn't have to clink a cup or wave his hands for silence. They were all still there, waiting. He took a deep breath, cleared his throat and began to speak.

"Spider MacCormack has had a freak accident. It looks like he might have been trying to climb up and reach for something overhead and lost his balance. We don't know how it happened or the extent of his injuries, but as soon as we do, we'll let you know. We've notified his parents, and they are on their way to him right now. Our Chaplain, Olympia Brown, went with him in the ambulance. She'll stay until his parents get there. There's nothing any of us can do right now except send him strength and courage. There was supposed to be an orientation tonight, but I think it's best if we hold off on that for now. If some of you want to stay and talk, Ellie and I will grab some coffee, and you can join us in the Fireplace Room next door.

There was a general shuffling of feet and scraping of chairs along with a hushed rumble of conversation as most of the people in the room moved toward the exits. Among them was Derek Jamison, who started toward the door but then turned back and approached Brad and Ellie with a worried expression on his face.

"Is there anything else you can tell me about what happened to Spider? I'm supposed to be the crew boss, and this happened on my watch. I feel responsible, like maybe I missed something or … I don't know." He shook his head and threw up his hands.

"Accidents happen, Derek. I know you're concerned and upset, but you can't be everywhere at once any more than I can. It happened on my shift, too. I can tell you he's in good hands, and we'll let you and everyone else know the minute we hear anything at all. I'm afraid that's the most and the best I can say right now."

Derek didn't look convinced, but he eventually nodded an agreement. "Thanks, Brad. I should probably go check in with the guys. They're all pretty upset."

"Good thinking, Derek."

When he left, Brad and Ellie were joined by only four members of the crew staff, two young men and two young women. As they made their way to the coffee urn and on to the Fireplace Room, Ellie whispered under her breath, "Have you thought about how Olympia's going to get back here?"

He clapped his free hand to his forehead. "Oh, gosh, in the madness of everything happening at once, I didn't give it a thought. I can go, or I can send somebody for her. Plenty of people stay up late around here."

"I'll go," said Ellie.

Six

Olympia felt it her duty to stay on at the hospital until Spider's parents arrived. She wouldn't want one of her sons left alone in a circumstance like this. She knew she couldn't tell them very much other than what she'd observed in the ambulance. Anything more would be up to the doctors and then, very likely, a psychiatrist. If she were in that situation, God forbid, she'd want to know every single detail. As a divorced mother of two grown sons, she'd been on more than one middle-of-the-night hospital run with one of the other of them when they were younger. But broken arms and dog bites were minor inconveniences compared to what these poor parents would soon be facing. Minister or mother, she could do no less than help comfort and reassure a frantic parent.

Once Spider was stabilized, they allowed Olympia to come back into the room and stay with him as long as he remained unconscious, but if he showed any signs of waking she was to call for a nurse at once.

She sat in the visitor chair beside the bed and looked at him lying there. He was pale as death and just as still. She so wanted to stroke his forehead, but that was out of the question. In his condition a strange touch, however well intended, could actually frighten him.

He was, as Brad had described, painfully thin. His breathing was labored and rasping, but at least, thank heaven, he was breathing—not fully on his own yet, but with bright green tubes of oxygen plugged into his nostrils and wires to several monitors hooked up to various parts of him, helping him to do so. She could see bruises darkening around his jaw and throat under the neck brace and thought about what had happened. Dear God, why?

The young man in the bed was a mystery. She'd never met him before, and yet here she was sitting beside him in a hospital emergency room, waiting for his parents to arrive. What then? What could she say? That he'd climbed up on something in his room and lost his balance. But why was he up there in the first place? That was the part she couldn't speak of, but she knew someone would have to.

Her thoughts were interrupted by a strangled grunt from the young man on the bed. His eyes fluttered open, and he began to struggle. Olympia hit the call button, took his hand in hers and began talking to him in as calming a manner as she could summon.

"Spider, you're in a hospital. You've had an accident, but you're going to be all right. You're safe here, and there are people to help you and take care of you. I'm the chaplain from Orchards Cove. I rode in the ambulance with you. Don't try and move, or you'll hurt yourself. I've called for a nurse."

Still he struggled, grunting and gasping, until the nurse came into the room. She called him by name, checked his vitals and told him she was glad he was awake, and she'd call for the doctor. Then, in a firm voice, she told him that his parents were on their way, and because of his neck injuries, he shouldn't try to move or talk. When he was visibly calmer, she turned to Olympia.

"Can you stay on with him until his parents arrive? They might need a chaplain when they get here."

"Of course," said Olympia, and this time she did follow her natural impulse and gently placed her hand on his damp forehead. As she did this he closed his eyes, and she could feel him begin to relax. Poor baby, she thought, tears welling up in her own eyes, what in the world has brought you to this, and will I or anyone else ever find out? "Please, God," she whispered under her breath, "watch over him."

It took another hour for Spider's parents to get there. The attending nurse introduced her to them, explaining that Olympia was the camp chaplain and the one who rode with him in the ambulance. The hollow-eyed couple thanked her and then turned as one to comfort their hurting child. Olympia scribbled her name and contact information on a sheet of paper and handed it to them as she slipped out of the room.

Olympia and Ellie got back to The Cove a little before one in the morning. They went straight to Brad's cottage and, after telling him all they could about Spider, which really wasn't very much, Olympia gratefully accepted Ellie's invitation to bunk down in the extra bedroom in her cottage, also known as the camp infirmary. It would have been a long dark walk back to her tent at the edge of the woods, and Olympia simply wasn't up to it. With a weary smile and still fully clothed minus her shoes, she fell back onto the bed and dragged up a blanket. She lay still and stared at the ceiling, wishing she could find a way to turn off her mind as easily as she could switch off the bedside lamp.

Eventually, sleep did come, but it was an uneasy sleep that gave her no rest. Olympia was badly shaken by what happened. Questions of why and what, if anything, she could do to help were overridden by the fact that she'd probably never know anything more about it. It was likely she'd never see or hear from Spider ever again. No doubt he'd be required to have a period of in-hospital psychiatric observation and evaluation followed by what? Therapy, drugs, both, none? His parents were understandably distraught, but after offering what words of comfort she could, standing with them beside his bed, she knew she'd likely never see them again either. They had been politely grateful, but it was clear they wanted to be alone with their son, and she totally understood. She'd feel the same herself. Before she left, she encouraged them to be strong for one another and said she'd keep them all in her prayers.

But the day would come when Olympia would learn the whole truth. She just couldn't know that yet. When she did, no one, least of all summer chaplain, single mother and ambivalent college professor Olympia Brown, could have been prepared for the consequences.

The next morning Olympia was not her best self. In addition to the grogginess due to the lack of sleep she was deeply concerned about Spider MacCormack. She wondered how he was doing and if she would ever learn what was so awful in his life that he couldn't face living any longer. Suicide was an act of desperation from which, if accomplished, there would never be any return.

She thought about his parents. Did they know how unhappy he was, and if they did, had they tried to help? Her motherly heart ached in sympathy for them. Olympia had a maternal heartache of her own, one she never talked about, and it was times like this, when she was feeling both helpless and powerless in the face of human tragedy, that it hurt the most.

She shuddered as she thought of her own two sons and how she would feel if either of them attempted—or worse, succeeded—at such a terrible act. Then she thought of her daughter, the one she'd been forbidden ever to talk about, the baby she'd given birth to and given up for adoption when she was only seventeen. What about her? Don't go there, Olympia, there's no point.

She forced her thoughts back to the present and pondered what this new day would be like. What would she be called upon to do in the face of the events of the night before? What could she do? What would they let her do? Whatever any of this might be, she would start by going back to the campsite for a shower and a change of clothes. After that she would find herself a large cup of coffee. After that, who knew?

That same morning, before the sounding of the breakfast bell, Brad Davies called an impromptu meeting of the maintenance and housekeeping staff, known as The Crew, in the common room of their dorm. Management didn't usually enter here. By unspoken agreement this was private crew space. Each year the current group redecorated it with sidewalk and dumpster scavengings, favorite posters and scraps of carpet. Some years they put up real window curtains brought from home. Other years they scoured thrift shops and yard sales for their finishing touches. It was part of the bonding process and as much a part of their summer ritual as short-sheeting a newcomer's bed or putting clear plastic wrap over the top of one of the toilet bowls. Summer pranks were as old as dirt, and every year they still managed to pull off a few surprises. It was part of the Cove tradition, and it was intended to be good fun.

Brad knocked on the door and waited to be invited in. Mostly college aged young men and women, many still in their pajamas, sat in anxious clusters, waiting to hear the latest word on Spider. Gone was their customary companionable banter, replaced by whispered questions, nervous throat clearing and the scuffling, shifting sounds of people who were ill at ease.

Brad cleared his own throat and tried not to fidget. He was nervous and out of his depth, but that was the last thing he wanted to convey to any of them. Right now they needed support and direction. This he could provide. He stuffed his hands into his pockets and began to speak.

"I called the hospital this morning and spoke with Spider's parents. The good news is that he's going to be OK."

This caused an immediate ripple of chatter followed by a palpable lessening of the unhappy tension in the room. Brad continued.

"The doctors say he'll need a few days more to get back on his feet and then some time in rehab before he can go home."

More chatter and affirmative head-nodding.

"That's the good news. Sadly for us, it's been decided that he should probably take the whole summer off, and therefore he won't be returning to work here. That means some of you will have to double up on jobs until we can get a replacement."

A collective sigh wove itself around and through them. Then came the inevitable questions.

"What happened?"

"Do you think that if we …?"

"Can we go see him?"

"Should we send him a card or something?"

Brad held up his hands, and they quieted down.

"I'll tell you what. Yes to the card, something big and cheery. After breakfast a couple of you can go over to the craft shop and see what you can come up with. We can all sign it, and I'll take it up there myself. After I've seen him and talked to him myself, I'll know better how he's doing and

I can tell you more of what happened and when or if he can have visitors."

There was a general nodding and affirmative smiling, followed by a ripple of youthful chatter, which in turn was interrupted by the clanging of the five-minute warning bell for breakfast.

Perfect timing, thought Brad. He gave them a grateful thumb's up and then turned and let himself out of the room.

Seven

Olympia squared her shoulders, crossed the road and started up the hill toward the dining hall. Her hair was still damp from the shower and felt pleasantly cool against her scalp, and her grumbling stomach reminded her she was more than ready for breakfast. The morning was warm and misty, but when the sun, now a pale white disc behind the cloying fog, burned through, it was likely to be a hot and humid day.

That was the meteorological weather taken care of, but what about the emotional weather? What would today be like after the events of last night? How much did the rest of them know about what really happened with Spider? His sad face haunted her. Was it in anyone's interest to tell them—or not to tell them? That particular question was not hers to answer, at least not right now.

She knew that temporary communities like this one bonded quickly, and something that affected one of them eventually affected all of them in one way or another. But a person didn't reach the point of attempting suicide in the space of few days. So what was going on in Spider's life before he came up here? Did he have any kind of history with any of the others? Many of them had been coming up here for years. Was he one of them, or was he a newbie? Did anyone know anything about him, and if so, who?

In truth, she wasn't sure how much of this was her concern. His personal life, however troubled, was not going to be anybody's business now or in the future. Her task would be to deal with the day-to-day needs of the conference center in view of what had happened. That would be enough to keep anyone busy.

She was a minister, not a detective, she told herself, and right now she was a minister who was ready for breakfast. Still, she couldn't deny her basic nature which was to feed the hungry, clothe the naked and protect the wayward and lost souls who somehow managed to find the well-worn path to her door. It had ever been thus. Perhaps it was partly due to her personal loss and her private atonement for what she'd done so long ago that she continually found herself reaching out to help every lost puppy and kitten she encountered. Would she ever know?

Olympia was so lost in thought that she didn't hear the person fall in next to her until she heard a woman's voice ask if she were the summer chaplain.

"Huh? What? Oh, sorry, I was a million miles away." Olympia stopped and looked at the woman standing beside her and held out her hand. "Hi. I'm Olympia Brown, and yes, I am the summer chaplain. What's your name?"

"Paula Budreau, I'm on the housekeeping crew. I wanted to come and talk with you and Brad last night after supper, but I felt sort of stupid because I didn't know anyone. Everybody seems to know each other, but this is my first time working here."

"Hi, Paula. I haven't been here in a long time, and then it was only once or twice in the distant past. I was never on staff before, so it feels like a first time for me, too."

Paula smiled, and the two women continued walking side by side up the slight incline toward the dining hall. As they crested the hill, the second, now-or-never, bell clanged, and more and more people followed the irresistible scents of bacon and fresh coffee. Olympia paused and turned to the woman standing next to her.

"Was there something in particular you wanted say last night?"

Paula nodded. "I still feel kind of dumb saying anything at all. I mean, I only got here a couple of days ago, and I don't know how things really work, but ..."

"But what?"

"Well, it was the first night we all got here. Spider was the first one to make friends with me. Everybody else on the crew seemed like they were old friends, you know, hugging and talking, and there I was off by myself in a corner. Nobody even looked in my direction. He was the only one who came over and talked to me. He was really sweet, but I could tell there was something wrong. He was smiling with his mouth, but his eyes were sad. He stayed with me for most of the evening and even introduced me to a couple of other people."

Olympia snapped into full focus and stepped out of the breakfast line. She gently moved Paula to a corner of the foyer where, despite the proximity of people passing by, they would not be overheard. The white sound made by lots of people talking was a perfect privacy curtain. Olympia thought of it as crowd cover. She'd made use of it before, sort of hiding out in plain view.

"Did something happen that night?"

She shrugged her shoulders. "It was weird. We were all getting ready to close up and go to bed when the crew boss, Derek, came over to us and said, 'Hi there, Spider-man, you riding a different bike tonight?' Then he sort of punched him in the shoulder. It looked like a regular guy-type buddy punch, but I could tell it hurt, only Spider didn't say anything."

Olympia didn't like the image that was forming in her mind. "Why do you think Derek did that?"

Paula shook her head. "I don't know. I asked Spider what that was all about, but all he said was that Derek picks on people and warned me not to get on his bad side."

"I appreciate your telling me this, Paula."

"I wouldn't have said anything at all except Spider was nice to me, and then he had this accident and got hurt, and I feel bad for him. You won't tell anyone I said it, will you?"

Olympia didn't like to lie, so she said only, "I can't imagine it being of any significance, but should that ever be the case, I give you my word that I won't use your name."

Paula responded with a grateful smile, and the two joined the rest of the crew and staff following their noses to the food that awaited them.

Derek Jamison stayed behind in the crew shack when Brad and the others left the building. When he was sure he was alone, he turned and went back into the room Spider had shared with three other crew members. Other than the fact that the dresser he'd climbed on had been removed, and his bed was stripped of bedding, nothing looked unusual or out of order. Spider's clothes were still jumbled in his locker, and there was a pair of well-used sneakers still sitting under the bed as if they were waiting for him to come back.

Derek walked quietly around the room, looking for anything that might give someone an idea of what really happened. He took one more look at the empty bed and then lifted the mattress. Nothing there. He shrugged his shoulders and slipped out of the room. He'd had a long and restless night. A good breakfast and then a job that needed doing would make him feel better. Derek needed to keep active.

Olympia left Paula outside the dining room and went over to the staff table with Brad and the others. They picked at their food, and as much as they tried to do otherwise, the conversation kept returning to Spider and what on earth had happened to make him do what he did. By now they all knew the truth, and much of the discussion was about what and how much to tell the crew.

It wasn't long before Olympia found herself in the familiar position of minister/counselor. The staff members were struggling with their own feelings, as well as the larger issue of the morale of the group as a whole after such a tragedy. Add to that the discomforting truth that one of the crew had been so deeply troubled that he tried to take his own life right in their very midst, and they'd missed it. What could and should they do, and what did they need to do to move on? How could they help the family? Most immediately, how could they support the rest of the crew, knowing that in less than a week the regular summer conference programs would begin?

Watching the anxiety and tension within his staff spiraling upward, Brad Davies made an executive decision. He put down his coffee cup and held up his hands in the time-out signal. When he had their attention, he spoke in a voice just loud enough to be heard but not overheard.

"I think we have too much hearsay and opinion and not enough factual information here. May I suggest we suspend this conversation for the time being and continue it later in the privacy of my office? I think it would be better for all concerned. I know the hospital won't give me any detailed information over the phone, which is why I've decided to go up there myself and see what I can learn firsthand. It's worth a shot. Until then, if any of the crew members ask about Spider, just say that we still don't know the cause and full extent of the injuries but as soon as we do, we'll let everyone know. Meanwhile, let's try and get back on track as far as the conferences go. There's still a lot to get done. The more normal we look and act, the better everyone is going to feel."

"Amen to that," said a relieved Olympia. This was followed by nods and murmurs of agreement and the clatter of cutlery and dishes as the people seated around the table rediscovered their appetites and tucked into their breakfasts.

Olympia had the morning free of official duties until the staff meeting at eleven in Brad's office. She thought about using the time to check out the Cove's outdoor chapel but scrapped that in favor of making a quick dash into town to purchase a few things for herself and the cats. While there, she planned to pick up a local newspaper or two and see what, if any, social improvement opportunities might be out there just waiting for her.

One of her self-imposed improvement projects for that summer was to spice up, or at least lightly season, her moribund social life. This was not something she felt comfortable doing anything about closer to home and work. Not that anyone she knew begrudged her dating or having a boyfriend, but if she were to be honest with herself, she'd been spectacularly unsuccessful in that department and had mixed emotions about trying again.

Now, given how long it had been since she'd even had a cup of coffee with a potential gentleman friend, she found herself uncharacteristically nervous and self-conscious about the prospect. However, with a whole summer away from home, far away from the curious eyes and ears of her children, her colleagues and gossipy neighbors, Olympia smelled opportunity in the air.

Today she planned to find herself a newspaper or magazine that carried local personal ads. In the event that she did find a suitable prospect, she knew it would not be as easy to connect with him as it would be if she were at home with her own private telephone and mailbox. However, this was the anonymity she needed for her first time out of the stable. Hope springs eternal, she told herself as she quick-stepped back to her tent to check on the cats and get her purse. Olympia had a job to do for the next ten weeks—two jobs, really. One was to be the chaplain she had been hired to be, to care for the community and, more specifically, to help with the aftermath of Spider's unfortunate accident.

The second job, the one that didn't pay money but offered far greater rewards in the long run, was getting herself a life. With the scent of change in the air, she realized that it had been way too long since she'd had one worth talking about. It was time to climb out of the rut that had served her and her sons, Randall and Malcolm, so well over the years of their growing up. Now that they were virtually out of the nest, returning home mostly to do laundry, borrow money or beg a home-cooked meal, she needed to get out of the nest as well. Today she would take the first step.

Olympia swung herself up into the driver seat of her much beloved vintage Volkswagen minibus and pushed the key into the ignition slot.

"Look out, world. Here I come, like it or not. There's a middle-aged lady with a wandering eye ready to … ready to do what?" she asked the rear-view mirror. "Well, we'll just wait and see, won't we?" replied the mirror.

Eight

In less than an hour Olympia was back in the sun-dappled privacy of her campsite. There was nothing she wanted more than to hunker down at the picnic table in the woods with a fresh cup of coffee and her newly purchased newspapers. Opportunity teased and beckoned, but duty called, and at 11:00 a.m. she was seated with the other members of the professional staff in Brad Davies' un-air-conditioned office. She hoped they would learn more of the circumstances surrounding what had happened the night before and, more specifically, how she might be called upon to help.

Meanwhile, the predicted humidity was appalling and only added to the discomfort level in the crowded space. Silently she prayed that the inevitable thunderstorm this kind of weather eventually produced would not be too long in coming.

Despite the ceiling fan belting away on high, the space below it was damp and airless. Brad had thoughtfully provided a huge beaker of cold lemonade for them all, but within five minutes Olympia's shirt was sticking to her back, and her glasses were fogging up. Brad smiled uncertainly and began to speak.

"Thanks for being so prompt, everybody. I'll try and keep it short. I've been to see Spider."

In response to their questioning looks, he continued. "As it turned out I was able to see Spider and talk to his parents. That was a mixed blessing, I'll tell you."

He grimaced and shook his head. "Poor kid. He looks awful. You can only imagine how his folks are feeling. I do know they were really grateful that I actually took the time to turn up. That's the good news, but I came away not knowing much more than when I arrived. I did learn he will be all right physically. That's something, at least. The parents are desperate for answers, and right now Spider isn't saying very much. I suppose that's understandable. Anyway, I was able to sit with him and tell him that we are all concerned and sending healing thoughts. Then I asked if there was anything specific that had happened here at the Cove to upset him so terribly."

"What did he say?" asked Ellie. She was wearing her camp nurse whites, white shirt and shorts and sneakers. The only touch of color was her turquoise and fuchsia socks. Over the years her wildly colored socks had become her trademark, and she played it to the hilt.

"It was really troubling. His parents had stepped out of the room for a moment, and maybe because of that he felt able to talk. He looked up at me and said, 'I'm skinny and geeky, and there's nothing I can do to change that. I'm really sick of being picked on and made fun of. It's nothing new. I should be used to it by now. But last night, just the thought of going into the dining room with, uh, everyone. I just couldn't do it. Something snapped. Now look at me. I'm such a fuck-up, I couldn't even get that right.'"

"Poor guy, what a shame," said Katie Simon.

"That's not the worst of it, "said Brad. "When I asked him if anyone or anything in particular had bothered him or made him feel unwelcome here, his answer was, 'Everybody and nobody.' He added that he'd thought that by coming to a church conference center, maybe things would be different, but it didn't work out that way. Then he shut down and wouldn't say any more. He wasn't really making sense. He never said what he was trying to get away from, but now that I think of it, he was probably pretty heavily medicated."

"I wonder what he meant about things being different? asked Olympia. The condensation on her glass of lemonade was dripping into her lap. She welcomed the coolness and held the wet glass to her temple.

Brad rubbed his chin. "No clue. Like I said, it was clear he wasn't going to say any more. He thanked me for coming and said he was tired. I took the hint and told him that if there was anything I could do right then or in the future, I was a phone call away, and I hoped one day he'd make the call."

"So something might have happened to him here, or just as likely, this was building long before he got here, and it all came together and pushed him over the edge," said Katie. She had a troubled frown on her face and was twisting her hands in concern.

"The pity is we may never know, because he's not coming back." Brad was shaking his head in obvious frustration. "But one thing we can do is to be extra vigilant when it comes to the rest of the crew—and the conferees, for that matter. I don't mean spying or anything but simply being aware if someone is being left out or seems to be having trouble fitting in. We're supposed to be welcoming and inclusive here, and we'd damned well better be that way ourselves. You know, role models practicing what we preach and all that." Brad was feeling distressed and angry, and it was beginning to show.

Olympia didn't blame him, but she wasn't ready to let the matter drop. She was remembering her conversation with Paula Budreau earlier that morning and wondering if that particular event, an underserved and humiliating punch to the shoulder, could have been a contributing factor or even the pivotal factor. Kids could be so fragile, not to mention mean. Why was that?

"Brad, have you or any of the rest of you, for that matter, had an opportunity to observe the crew's interactions with each other?" In response to his puzzled look she added, "Spider was terribly self-conscious about his looks and lack of social skills. He told me as much when I was sitting with him, waiting for his parents to arrive. Kids can be really cruel, even church conference center kids who are supposed to know better."

"What are you suggesting, Olympia?"

"Not so much suggesting as inquiring. One or two isolated events don't usually drive someone to make an attempt on his or her own life, but ongoing humiliation and physical abuse, especially if other kids pick up on it and start to join in, can be devastating. You know, the pack animal mentality, surrounding and attacking the weakling. Kids who are strong and have a good sense of self can often throw this kind thing off. But those who for whatever reason, be it personality, past events, family issues, who are dealing with more than the everyday teenage angst and insecurity can be at risk and not even know it until it's too late."

"Do think that's what may have happened with Spider?" asked Ellie.

Olympia chewed on her lip for a moment before responding. "I don't know what to think. I only know I'm very troubled by it. We don't really know anything about his past or if he has history with any of the people here. The truth is, it's probably no longer our business, but I can't simply walk away from it just because he didn't actually die on our watch."

Ellie leaned forward. She was looking more and more troubled. "If something happened here that was a contributing factor, and we missed it, does that make us partly responsible? Young people come here to have a positive social and spiritual outdoor experience. That didn't happen for Spider."

"No," said Olympia, "it most certainly didn't."

"So when are we going to tell everyone the full story? We have to, you know."

Brad looked acutely uncomfortable. "I was hoping we could avoid that, Ellie, but you're right, we have no choice. My main priority is getting this place up and running, and the clock is ticking. Spider's actions were nothing less than tragic, no question about that, but I have a job to do, and your jobs all depend on my doing mine."

"I have a thought," said Olympia.

"Let's hear it. I can tell you I damn sure don't have any right now."

Olympia felt herself again slipping into pastoral mode. She spoke with a calm assurance that was second nature to her in these situations.

"There's no doubt that we need to tell the crew the whole story, or as much of it as we know ourselves, and the sooner we do it the better. Keeping secrets is bad for an organization. I suggest we call a staff meeting for after lunch today, tell them the full extent of what happened and give everyone a chance to react and respond. If you want, you can say I'm available if any of them are in need of a chaplain to help sort out their feelings. Some may want a more private and confidential setting."

Olympia recalled talking with Paula Budreau earlier that day, and even before that, the conversation over the phone with Brad before she had come here. Hadn't he said that Derek could be rigid and demanding? What about that? She decided to speak to him privately about that rather than start any rumors.

Then she had another and much more serious thought. She decided not to share this one with anyone, at least not until she had a chance to confirm or disprove her suspicions. She uncrossed her legs and sat straighter in her chair.

"It's likely none of us will have a chance to talk with Spider again, but I would be interested in hearing what the others say after they hear the full story. If something was going on here that we might have been able to prevent, or can prevent from happening again, I think we need to know it."

"You know, Olympia, you said it yourself, this likely wasn't a one-off. He was probably teetering on the edge when he came up here, and we didn't know it." It was clear that Brad was beginning to feel defensive.

"Very true, Brad, but if we do discover that something or someone here was a contributing or an exacerbating factor, we should try to find out what it was. It's important for Orchards Cove as an institution now and in the future."

Brad looked miserable; he was picking at his fingernails and biting his lower lip. "What the hell do I say? This wasn't in the job description."

Real life rarely is, thought Olympia. "Maybe you shouldn't be the one doing the talking, Brad. Ellie is the medical person here. She could be the one to give the medical facts. After that, we all take questions, and then you offer my services as a chaplain. I don't think we should make an afternoon of it. It should be brief, to the point and then be done. An event like this can become a morbid sort of cause célèbre within the group, and they can take it all out of proportion. I say we should be compassionate but matter of fact. Tell them there is nothing more we can do here and assure them that Spider is in good hands. From there you tell them we need to get on with the business at hand, and we'll update them if we learn anything new."

Brad looked visibly relieved. "Perfect. Thank you, Olympia. Ellie, are you OK with that approach?"

She nodded. "I think it makes good sense. I can do it. As long as we seem confident about what we're saying and doing, the crew will pick up on it. I believe it's referred to as a united front."

Brad blew out a long sigh of relief and looked at his watch. "Thanks, everyone. We have a few minutes before the lunch bell rings. I don't know about the rest of you, but I need to run off a little energy. My neck and shoulders feel like there are iron bands in there instead of muscles."

"It's been a totally exhausting twenty-four hours for all of us," said Olympia.

Nurse Ellie stood and peeled her wet camp shirt away from her chest and back. "And it ain't over yet," she whispered under her breath.

Nine

After the lunch meeting with Brad, Derek Jamison, in his role as crew boss, called a meeting of his own in the crew shack. When they were all there he stood and waved both hands to get their attention. His stance was deliberately relaxed, but his eyes, darting back and forth, told the real story.

"Look, guys, I'm not saying we could have done anything to stop Spider, but I'm getting the idea that Brad thinks it's something we did that might have set him off."

"Or maybe something we didn't do," muttered Paula Budreau under her breath.

"What was that?" Derek shot her a dark look.

"Nothing. Just thinking out loud. He seemed so lonely."

Derek's expression hardened. "People make their own way in this world, Paula. He could have done more to help himself. He just couldn't be bothered."

"I agree with Paula, I think we should have tried a little harder to include him," said Miguel Dos Santos, a slightly overweight college sophomore who was slouched beside Paula.

"Easy for you to say, but we have a job to do. I have a job to do. We were hired to make this place run, not just hang out and party all the time. People are depending on us."

"That doesn't mean we can't have fun while we work," said Paula.

Derek crossed his arms. "You can have fun after your work is done. Brad and that chaplain woman are …"

"Her name's Olympia Brown," said Paula. "She's nice. I like her."

Another even darker look. "Brad and Olympia told us to keep our eyes and ears open, no more than that. I'm taking Brad at his word. This is a conference center, not a psych-ward. Look, I'm just as upset as you all are about what happened with Spider, but to be honest, it's better he's out of here than freaking out on us every other day. We don't need that."

"But …"

"But nothing, Paula. You've got work to do, I've got work to do. We're a good team, and we get the job done. That's what they are paying us for. Leave the group therapy to the shrinks, OK?"

"If you say so," said Paula, pushing herself up out of the dilapidated sofa. "Meanwhile, I have some toilets to clean. So if you don't mind, I'll just go do my job. The atmosphere is much better there."

"Meeting adjourned, "snapped Derek.

Later that afternoon Olympia was sitting at her picnic table with a limp newspaper in front of her. The cloying humidity had wilted everything and everyone. Even the cats were listless. She was holding a glass of cold water in her left hand and slowly running a finger through a section of personal ads with the other. While she wasn't free of concern for Spider, she was confident that she and the others had done all they could do for the present, and anything that might happen in the future was out of their control. The meeting with the crew kids had gone well. They were understandably shaken. Many expressed concern and asked if they could have done more and what, if anything, they could do now.

"Be mindful and observant," is what she told them and went on to say that it was very likely Spider was troubled and unhappy long before he arrived at Orchards Cove.

She explained that in a community such as this, it's all of our responsibility to look out for one another within reason. Not as in spying or controlling, but in being generous and compassionate while working together and accepting one another's strengths and weaknesses. At the end of the meeting she did caution them that if there was problem they didn't feel they could handle, it was important to speak to one of the senior staff—in complete confidence, of course.

A few of them did ask to speak with her privately, and she agreed to arrange meetings with them on the following morning, schedules permitting. What she didn't say was that she was allowing time to let their see-sawing emotions settle down and get things into proper perspective. All that being said, the first to put her name on the on the appointment list was Paula Budreau. Stop obsessing, Olympia scolded herself. What will be, will be, and I can't do one more thing about any of this right now. She wiped the sweat from the back of her neck. She could actually feel the barometric pressure dropping as the very air around her seemed to grow greenish and darken. She could smell that eerie, sweet-scented, heavy calm that precedes a hell-for-leather thunderstorm. Even the birds had stopped their treetop conversations and seemed to be waiting for something.

She turned another limp page of the paper and smoothed it with her free hand as a low growl of thunder gave warning of the impending storm. Not a minute too soon, she thought. I don't think I could stand another five minutes of this humidity. Olympia counted the seconds between the first rumble and the next and wondered if she should stay in her tent or make a run up the hill for the dining hall porch and watch the storm come in over the ocean. Olympia loved watching storms, even if they did scare the hell out of her.

A louder, more immediate, crash answered her question: neither. She scooped up her paper, hoisted the cat cage with both hands and made straight for the safety of the campground social hall just as another flash of lightning, crack of thunder and the first fat drops came blasting out of the sky.

It was one of those sudden outbursts, quick and violent and potentially very dangerous. Olympia watched as the wind picked up dramatically, and torrential rain began to fall, at first straight down and then horizontally. This was not good. She had wisely positioned herself and the terrified cats well away from the door and as far into the back corner of the building as she could. She knew the heavily cross-beamed corners would be structurally stronger than the unsupported open space in the middle. She hunkered down and waited.

Because it was still pre-season, there were no other residents in the campground, and she was totally alone. She hadn't told anyone exactly what she was doing that afternoon, and as far as any of them knew she could be anywhere from Portsmouth to Portland or beyond. Another crash of thunder boomed. The rain was coming down so hard now that Olympia couldn't see anything past the water-soaked screens, and for one of the few times in her life that she could remember, she was actually beginning to feel nervous. The cats were uncharacteristically silent, but their big eyes and flattened ears spoke volumes.

The thunder and lightning were virtually simultaneous now, and a rapidly widening pool of rainwater was flooding in through the windows and screen door on the windward side of the building. Olympia ventured out of her corner only long enough to drag one of the old wooden picnic tables back to where she and the cats could still be safe and relatively dry. As she sat cross legged on top of the table, making soothing noises to the animals, she was also mentally taking note of where all the leaks in the roof were located. This would be a job for Derek and the crew. By focusing on locating and counting the leaks, Olympia could almost think she wasn't as anxious as she really was. Then came a lull, but the silent air around her was electric. She could actually feel it in her hair. The wind dropped, and the rain seemed to lessen. Olympia held her breath. Then a ferocious crash of thunder accompanied the flash of blue-white lightning which hit and split one of the stately old pines that stood immediately next to the building in which she and the cats had sought shelter.

The next sound she heard was that same tree crashing through the roof, trapping the three of them in one of the two corners of the building that remained standing. Both cats hissed, but their protests were totally lost in the sounds of cracking boughs and groaning roof timbers. Olympia watched and listened as the hard rain poured freely through the jagged hole which had once been the roof and expanded the small lake widening out to the area beneath the legs of Olympia's perch.

No way in hell was she going to move from where she was. Her mother had repeatedly warned her of the perils of downed wires, electrified puddles and strange men, and even if she wasn't sure any such danger existed here and now, she wasn't about to risk it—the puddles anyway. She still had her newspaper, crumpled but readable, and one way or another she was willing, if not actively looking forward to, taking a chance on a strange man or two. It had been a long and dry several years, and even in the midst of one hell of a rain storm, middle-aged hope still springs eternal.

Meanwhile, over and around her, the rain was stopping, and glimpses of sun and sky were visible through the hole in the roof. But clearing skies or not, she and the cats were not moving until someone in charge sounded an all clear. For lack of a better expression, the Reverend Doctor Olympia Brown and her two feline companions were literally and quite effectively tabled until further notice.

Ten

"Up the hill," which is how the Orchards Cove regulars referred to the oceanfront parcel of the complex on the other side of the road from the campground, staff and crew were beginning to emerge. They came, some dry, some dripping, from whatever shelter they had scrambled to. Now, almost as quickly as the vicious storm had come, it was gone. A bright sun burst forth, and a wary group of people began to survey the damage. From where they stood it was mostly downed branches and overturned wicker rocking chairs, but all of them had heard the one mighty crash down the hill and wondered what must have surely been hit. Early on in the deluge, Brad and Derek had the simultaneous thought to shut off the power to the entire complex. This way, if lightning did strike something, they wouldn't have to add electrical hazard to whatever damage might have been caused by the storm. Brad rang the dinner bell and assembled them on the weathered wrap-around porch of the dining hall. All but Olympia were present and accounted for.

"Does anyone know if Olympia went off campus this afternoon?" asked Brad after finishing the head count.

"Last I heard she was going down to her tent to chill out with the cats and the local newspaper," said Ellie.

Dereck stepped out of the huddle. "If her van is here, then we know she's here, but if she is, she's alone in the outermost site in the place. I tried to talk her out of it, but she said she needed peace and quiet. She should have listened. She could be in trouble."

Without another word, he turned and sprinted down the rain-soaked street, broad-jumping over branches and splashing through puddles. He barely paused at the cross walk and dashed across the street to the campground parking area, where he stopped because he could go no farther. Before him was utter chaos. Uprooted trees, flattened staff tents and upended picnic tables were in stark contrast to the bright, sunny sky and fresh breeze that stirred the tops of the still standing pines. Later he would learn that a microburst—a sudden, violent and site-specific tornado-like blast of wind and rain—had occurred only hundreds of feet from where they were all safely sheltered. He looked left and right and spotted Olympia's bright blue van at the far end of the lot. It was still wet and covered with pine branches, but from where he stood he could see no visible body damage. He ran over, hoping he would find her safe inside, but the van was empty and leaking water from all sides. The windows had been left open. If the staff tents had been ripped to shreds, what kind of condition was Olympia's tent going to be in? What kind of condition would the hardheaded chaplain be in, and where the hell was she? He should have insisted she take the spot he'd selected. Next time he would.

Derek turned back to the field, saw the shattered remains of the social hall and groaned out loud. The tree that had smashed through the roof was not the only one down, and the broken and uprooted tangle was blocking all paths to everything on site. It was going to take a bulldozer to get anywhere, never mind out to where Olympia's tent site, or what might be left of it, was located. Even though the temperature and the humidity were markedly lower, Derek was sweating. He liked the idea of being the hero who found the chaplain, but inside he was terrified of what he might find along the way. Spider's brush with death, plus his own internal fears were enough to make him very unwilling to be the first to find an injured or possibly dead person. So when in doubt, scream, he thought. From the safety of the parking lot he bellowed, "Olympia?"

From the heap of rubble across the field, came the reply. "I'm in the social hall with the cats! I'm OK, but I'm trapped!"

At that point Brad and the others arrived, and Derek no longer had to think for himself. He gestured grandly toward the remains of social hall and the fallen tree.

"I found her. She's in the social hall, or what's left of it. She's OK, but we can't get to her. We need a machine."

This time Brad was the one to address the crisis but not before he whispered, "Oh, thank God." Then he cupped his hands to his face and hollered, "Olympia, it's Brad! Stay where you are. We have to get a bulldozer. It might be a couple of hours. Can you hang on?"

Sitting cross-legged on top of her picnic table, Olympia thought, do I have a choice? The image of supper and maybe a very large glass of wine dissolved before her eyes. She wasn't hungry yet, just the opposite, but she would be. Right now she had the cats and water, if she needed it, puddles full of it. But the puddles might be live. Uh oh.

"What about power lines?" she screamed through the hole in the roof.

"No power, you're safe. We'll get you as soon as we can."

"I'm not going anywhere!"

Ellie, who had been quiet up until that moment, turned to the group. "Is there one of you who is willing to try and crawl through that mess with me? I don't want to do it by myself, and I don't want to leave Olympia out there alone. If a couple of us can get through, we should be able to get her back out. If we can't, we can at least wait in there with her."

"I've done some mountaineering; I'll give it a go," said Paula Budreau.

"We should bring some towels or something so she can dry off and not get a chill," said Ellie.

Derek was oozing confidence now. He was back in control, and Ellie and Paula were more than grateful for the assistance. "Let me go grab a hatchet and a bow saw from the garage. Hey, Brad, do you know if there's chain saw up the hill? We ought to be able to do it with that." He addressed Olympia again. "Hold tight! We're going to try and get through!"

"Be careful!" came her reply.

Brad wished them luck, cautioned them, and went off for the chain saw and then to try and locate some available heavy equipment. Not only did he have a chaplain to rescue, he had a conference season to open in three days. Brad needed more than a bulldozer. A miracle would come in handy right now, he thought, and wondered if he'd remembered to include that in Olympia's job description.

Several miles north of the mess at Orchards Cove, Spider MacCormack was sitting in the back of an ambulance on his way to a psychiatric hospital. Once there, he would undergo a thorough diagnostic evaluation and participate in a treatment program before he could be released into the care of his parents. Riding backward nauseated him, but he had little choice in the matter. It seemed he had little choice in anything these days, but that would all change once he got out. This whole thing, awful as it was, had taught him a thing or two about himself and the consequences of his actions. The next time he undertook a plan of action, he would not make a mess of it. That much he was sure of. He had time. He had all summer. Spider leaned back against the headrest and closed his eyes, shutting out the images flashing past the window and willing himself not to throw up.

Three hours after she'd been located, Olympia was a free woman. Still quite shaken, but walking on her own two feet, she was making her way back to dry land and civilization. Derek led the charge with Paula and Ellie close behind. As the three of them picked their way through the trees and branches, Derek held the cat carrier aloft. Olympia followed close behind him, while Paula and Ellie carried the tools and brought up the rear.

As is often the case after getting through a scary event, it was only now beginning to dawn on Olympia just how serious her situation had been—what might have happened but mercifully did not. As she threaded her way along behind Derek, she kept repeating calming words to the cats, but in reality, Olympia was trying to calm herself. Later they would go back and see what was left of her campsite, but not after a glass of wine, a cup of coffee or a lot of chocolate.

When she did go back, it was not a pretty sight. Many of her clothes had to be retrieved from puddles and bushes, but they could be washed and saved. Her lovely new tent and almost everything in it was history. However, a trip north to Freeport and a couple of laps around the L. L. Bean Outlet store with credit card in hand would take care of that, and the sooner the better. If she could borrow a car, she'd go off and get started that very afternoon.

Olympia always did have an eye for a bargain. If a couple of smudges or a ripped package meant she could save a few dollars, the good reverend was on it. It took less than two hours for her to be completely re-outfitted with enough money left over to treat herself to a better than bargain-bin bottle of wine and a fresh newspaper. The cats each got an official L. L. Bean catnip mouse and a new cat box. As was their custom, they received their gifts with mild disinterest until no one was looking. Then the two played themselves quietly senseless over the catnip and vigorously christened their new latrine.

Eleven

On Tuesday, three days after the storm that pretty much took out the Orchards Cove camp ground, most of the big mess was gone. Other than a few torn, ragged stumps that would be permanent testimony to what had taken place, the tree tangle had been cut up and dragged off or stacked for firewood. Over the next few days the picnic tables would be repaired, and those that were beyond hope would be cut up for firewood and replaced.

A benevolent benefactor donated a wedding tent. Although it had seen better days, it had both screened and plastic sides that could be dropped, if needed. This was carefully put up where the remains of the social hall had been demolished and removed. While not fully restored, Orchards Cove was open and ready for the first influx of conferees, an annual mid-week family conference from a local church. They'd been coming for years, knew the ins and outs of the place and understood the established routine better than most of the staff. It would make for an easy start. They would be forgiving of minor inconveniences, and most would cheerfully lend a hand, if necessary.

Olympia's duties would be minimal; these folks came with their own agenda and cast of characters. Weather permitting, she would do an ingathering service for them all in the pine-ringed woodland chapel, or what was left of it, and in the evenings she was asked to offer a simple service of evensong. It would appear to all and sundry that after a really rocky start, Orchards Cove was open for business and ready to go.

Olympia's mother had a saying for everything, and when a planned event got off on a bad—or in this case, disastrous—foot, she would chirp, "Poor start, good finish, you know." Olympia chuckled at the memory. If this was someone's idea of a poor start, then the rest of the summer should surpass all expectations in its promise of wonderfulness. Unfortunately, Olympia's mother was not always right in her predictions.

Still, the air was clear, the sun was shining, and the new conferees were coming in and setting up tents and pop-up campers. Children were scampering through the convivial chaos. One or two families even had recreational vehicles, but Olympia, camping snob that she was, considered that wimping, not camping, and she would have none of it. (Harrumph, so there!) Although, if she was going to be totally honest with herself, after being trapped in a free-fall tree-fall for several hours, she had given the idea of something more sturdy overhead more than a passing thought.

Finances, however, brought her back to reality. She could afford a tent, a good one, but no more than that. This new, larger tent was lightweight, had two windows and a floor and an even larger attached screen-house where the cats would have more room. It was palatial compared to the one she'd arrived with. Olympia was deservedly pleased with herself and her good fortune, and her pleasure was twofold. In the intervening days between her entrapment, courtesy of the storm, and the setting up of her new digs, she'd had a response from one of the singles ad writers she had contacted. A man who called himself John Stainer had left a message and a call back number in the camp office for her. Things were definitely looking up.

As she wandered across the field to the garage office where the campground pay phone lived, Olympia was feeling positively girlish. Instead of microbursts, fallen trees and a suicidal young man, she was thinking of pretty clothes and make-up and what this person might be like.

Then reality struck. Her present wardrobe, that which had survived the storm, consisted of shorts and jeans in various stages of the aging process, tee shirts torn and untorn, and two summer Sunday preaching outfits. These were two pairs of lightweight slacks, one black and one white, and two flowery, gauzy tunic-blouses which flowed artfully over and below her well-rounded behind. There was more: underwear (practical), rain gear, sensible modest pajamas (ancient), and a knee-length terry bathrobe for running to and from the outdoor showers. Not much allure there, she thought, but if need be, I'll go shopping.

Olympia smiled and dug in the pocket without the hole in it for the coins she'd collected to use in the phone. As a staff person, she was entitled to use the office phone, but doing that would broadcast to anyone within earshot what she was up to. Uh uh. She held on to the change in one hand while she fished in her back pocket for the scrap of paper with John Stainer's number. This was a first for Olympia, and she was surprised at how self-conscious she was feeling. Still, this is what she had said she wanted in her post fifty-year-old life, male companionship and maybe, hopefully, more than just companionship.

Finally, taking the pay phone in hand and pushing an assortment of coins into the slot, she took a deep breath, dialed the number and instantly considered hanging up before the first ring. But courage, determination and curiosity prevailed, and she listened to the rings until a male voice said, "Hello?"

"Uhhh, John Stainer?"

"Speaking. Who's calling?"

"You, uh, left a message for me. I responded to the personal ad you put in the *Sacco Community Reporter*, 'divorced white male, early fifties, fond of good books, good food, looking for interesting women of a similar age.' I'm Olympia Brown, and I think I'd like to meet you."

"Think?" He chuckled.

He has a pleasant voice, she thought. "No, I would like to meet you, really." She paused. What to say next? "Uh, by way of describing myself, in response to your ad I can say I'm an avid reader, I like both cooking and eating, and let's just say that people don't fall asleep in my company."

This produced a real laugh. "And you have a sense of humor."

"So I'm told. What kinds of books do you read?" she asked.

"Sci-fi and civil war history, mostly. Probably more sci-fi. I guess that's two ends of the rope, isn't it. What about you?"

At that point, the operator came on, demanding more money, and Olympia dutifully dumped some more coins into the slot.

"Are you calling from a pay phone? Where are you?"

"I am indeed. It's more private. I'm working in southern Maine for the summer. I don't know anyone up here and thought I would like to meet someone and go out once in a while. I don't socialize with people I work with. It's never a good idea."

She was carefully not telling him where in Maine she was working. That could come later, maybe.

"What do you do?"

Olympia hesitated. Should she tell him the truth, that she was a minister? Or should she just say she was on staff at a summer camp? Both were true.

"Cat got your tongue?"

What the hell, she thought, might as well jump in with both feet. "I'm working as a camp chaplain. I'm a minister."

"Ohhh." This was followed by silence on the other end of the line.

"Do you have a problem with that?"

"I don't know, I never thought about it. I guess I'm game to at least have a coffee and meet you in person."

Don't do me any favors, she thought with a scowl but said only, "Ministers put their shoes on one at a time, just like anyone else, and we do our own shopping, too."

He laughed more broadly this time. "Look, no offense, you just caught me off guard, that's all. I'm just afraid I'll slip and say the wrong thing. I'll do my best not to. Could we meet for lunch sometime next week?"

"Technically, I'm supposed to have Wednesdays off, that's tomorrow, but that's not good for me. How about next Wednesday, would that work for you?"

"Sure. I own my own business, so I have a flexible schedule. How far away are you from Portland?"

"About an hour, depending on traffic."

"There's a great little place right off the Portland exit. It's called the Gourmet Burger. It's well marked, and there's plenty of parking. How's one o'clock?"

Olympia decided to say nothing about being a vegetarian. She was used to managing this, even in burger joints.

"It does. How will I know you?" Let's see what he says to this, she thought.

"Hmmm, I'm average height, uh, I guess sort of middling weight, and I'll be wearing a Hawaiian shirt. How will I know you?"

For one irascible moment Olympia considered giving him a false description of herself so that she could check him out and then then simply leave if she didn't like what she saw.

"We must be twins," she quipped. "I'm in my fiftieth year, I have short salt-and-pepper hair and, like you, I'm of middling weight." Then she added, "I'll be wearing white slacks and a long flowery blouse."

"I thought ministers had to wear black."

"We can dress pretty much how we want during the week. Sundays, if I'm preaching, it's a different story, and that depends on where we're preaching. I'll tell you more about it when we meet, if you're really interested.

"I'm interested. Maybe I could come hear you preach sometime?"

Whoa, boy, she mouthed at the receiver. "Let's start with lunch, OK? One step at a time."

"OK, then I guess I'll see you in a week, give or take twenty-four hours."

When Olympia returned to her solitary camp site, since she still refused to move closer to the campfire circle, she had a spring in her step and a mischievous grin on her middle-aged face.

"That was step one," she told the trees. "Let's see what step two brings."

Twelve

As she rounded the last curve in the path she could hear the cats meowing a hungry greeting. They'd settled into their comfortable new digs very nicely and were now demanding to be fed again. Eventually she'd turn them loose and let them run around in the woods when she was there to keep an eye on them, but she didn't feel ready for that quite yet. After she'd fed them and checked the litter box, she settled into her new and improved aluminum camp chair, armed with her notebook and pencil. She had work to do. There was a Sunday service to plan plus some family-oriented evensong programs for the next two days. These were usually songs and stories on a theme, but such things didn't materialize out of thin air. Olympia was a planner who liked to have both her secular and ecclesiastical ducks and all of their paraphernalia lined up with their shoes polished and ready to go. The theme of the family conference was Who and What Makes a Family? That was easy enough—lots of material there. She'd no sooner opened her notebook when she heard the soft, even rhythm of approaching footsteps. So much for privacy, she thought, and looked up. It was a worried-looking Paula Budreau.

"Hi, Rev," she called out, flapping both hands in greeting.

Olympia gestured to the other new camp chair and set her notebook and pencil down on the carpet of sweet-scented pine needles that covered the ground.

"Have a seat."

Paula moved the chair so she was facing Olympia. Then she wiggled herself into a comfortable slouch and looked around. "It's nice back here. Pretty isolated, too, I'd say. You don't feel nervous or anything being out this far?"

Olympia smiled. Why did everyone seem so worried about her choice of real estate?

"I'm not at all that far away from everything, especially now that the conferences are starting up so I can actually see some of the other tents and campers. Close enough but not too close. I came up here for some think time, and it's really peaceful out here. Besides, I have the skunks and raccoons for company. I don't bother them, they don't bother me, and we all live together in close harmony." Olympia waved her fingers in the air and singsong-ed the last few words of her impromptu verse.

Paula laughed at the corny little rhyme, but then her face went all serious again as she reached into her shirt pocket and pulled out a folded envelope.

"I got a letter from Spider this morning, and I don't know what to make of it."

"What do you mean?" asked Olympia.

"Here, you read it and tell me what you think." Paula held out the letter.

She shook her head. "Mmm, I think I'd rather have you read it to me. If it was addressed to you, I wouldn't feel right reading it."

"OK, whatever." Paula shrugged, unfolded the letter and began to read.

Dear Paula, I'll bet you didn't expect to hear from me again. I'm doing much better, and if I keep taking the pills and doing what they tell me, I should be out soon—they won't tell me when. I had to agree to stay with my parents for the rest of the summer, but I'd like to see you again. Maybe we could go for a beach walk or something ... that is if you want to. You could call The Northeast Rehabilitation and Treatment Center and leave a message for me, or you could write me a letter. I'll be here for at least another week. You and the chaplain who came with me that night are the only good things about that place, and I need to hold on to that. Please let me know, and say hello to Olympia Brown for me. Love, Spider.

Olympia had enough experience in dealing with troubled people to know what she needed to do most was let the other person do the talking. This could be tricky.

"So, what do you think, Paula?"

"I'm wondering if I should go see him. I feel so bad about what happened."

"Do you want to visit him because you feel bad for him or because you like him enough to want to see him in spite of what happened?"

"Probably a little of each. Before ... the accident I was hoping he'd ask me out, so I guess I was starting to like him."

"What would be most comfortable for you right now?'

Paula paused and thought for a moment and then looked up. "I think writing to him. Hey, I could call and leave a message at the hospital saying I'm going to send him a letter. That's kind of doing both at once, isn't it?"

Olympia felt the tension in her neck and shoulders ratchet down by a couple of notches.

"I think that's a good idea, Paula. That way you'll be able to get a sense of how he's feeling through his letters. Then you can decide whether it's a good idea to go see him or to wait until he's feeling even better."

"Maybe I could just go up there and surprise him on my day off. I have a car. It's a junker, but it runs good enough."

Olympia shook her head. "I like your first idea better. Start with the phone message and a letter or two. Then you can see how he's doing. I think writing to him is a great idea. Getting a letter is such a treat; it will be something for him to look forward to. But you need to remember he's had a very serious and traumatic incident in his life, and it's going to take him a while to come back. This is a fragile time for him. Go slowly."

She looked thoughtful. "I didn't think of it that way, but now that I do, I suppose you're right."

"Take it one day at a time, Paula. My mother always said, 'Slow and steady wins the race.'"

"What's your mother like?" asked Paula.

"Different," said Olympia, and other than an exaggerated eye-roll, she didn't offer to say how or why that was so.

As Paula started to get up, Olympia had another thought and waved her back down. "Hold on a second. If or when you do write to Spider, tell him I was asking for him, will you, since he mentioned me in the letter? I felt so helpless sitting with him that night at the hospital. He needs to know people care about him, especially now."

"Sure," said Paula, "I'll be happy to."

After she left, Olympia tried to return to the task at hand but was interrupted once again. This time it was a scratching, scrabbling sound coming from behind one of the low bushes that ringed her campsite. She looked in that direction and saw a mother skunk and three babies emerge from the cover of the foliage. Don't move! She knew full well if you leave skunks alone, they will leave you alone, but in the present circumstances, with all four of the little darlings less than three feet from your own two feet, not even the bravest of women might be able to remember it. Nonetheless, she had no options. Earlier in the week she'd been tabled by a fallen tree, now she was being chaired by a mama skunk who was in search of food and taking her own sweet time looking around for it. After a leisurely tour of the immediate area offered nothing appetizing for the little family, they waddled back off into the deeper woods. Olympia allowed herself a giant sigh of relief. This is what I asked for, she reminded herself, and this is what I got. Mother always did tell me to be careful what I wished for.

Shut up in the claustrophobic telephone cubicle located outside the camp office, Paula Budreau was leaving a message for Spider MacCormack, saying she'd gotten his letter, was glad he was feeling better, and he should expect a letter real soon.

In the crew shack Derek Jamison was stretched out on the sofa in the common room, reading. He put down the book, looked up and scowled at the interruption as Miguel Dos Santos entered the room.

"How come you're not working? Finished already? What time is it?"

"Oh, hi, Derek, I didn't see you there. We had to stop. We ran out of paint."

"And there wasn't anything else you could find to do?"

"Not without checking with you or Brad first."

Derek liked the sound of that. He liked deference. He liked people to know who was boss. "Good thinking, Miguel, it's almost dinnertime anyway. I'll go get more paint in the morning. See you later."

Miguel was not being invited to join him in the comfort of the common room, he was being dismissed.

"If you don't mind, I think I'll hang out here until then. It's cooler in here than in my room."

"Suit yourself. "Derek turned a page in his book without looking up.

After leaving the message for Spider, Paula curled up in one of the old porch rocking chairs to write her letter. What do you say to someone who tried to kill himself, she wondered? Finally she settled on a newsy message, telling him about the storm, the trapped chaplain, the massive clean-up and how lucky he was to have missed it. She finished up by saying she was glad to hear he was getting better and how nice it would be to see him again, all relatively neutral topics.

Thus pleased with herself, she sealed it, added a stamp and dropped it in the camp outgoing mail basket where it would be collected the next morning. Then she took it right back and stuffed it in her pocket. Whoever picked up and sorted the mail would no doubt see it, and twenty minutes after that the whole place would know. Not a good idea. Later on she would walk down the street to the local convenience store where she knew there was a US Postal Service mail box. Much better idea.

Paula looked at her watch and realized why she was so hungry. It was time for crew supper. No bells were rung for the crew meals once camp was in session so as not to confuse the conferees. In the dining hall two tables near the entrance to the kitchen were set up just for them, and the heaping bowls and plates were already on the serving table when she arrived. The custom was that the first people in set the tables and got to pick where they sat. Last in had to clean up. The system worked well, and people were rarely late. Paula didn't mind either task, so she didn't rush.

The food here was plentiful, good and basic. With so many tastes to cater to and a nonprofit budget to work with, well-prepared comfort food in generous proportions was the order of the day. The salads and vegetables were always fresh and from local farms, when possible. The bread was homemade, and desserts were usually made from mixes but were still fresh and delicious. Chocolate cake with vanilla frosting was a perennial favorite, second only to ice cream. As they entered the dining hall, Paula caught the combined scents of garlic, tomato and cheese. It was spaghetti and meatball night, and for a fleeting moment she wondered what Spider might be having for supper.

Thirteen

At the same time Paula was tucking into her meal, Olympia, who was expected to eat with the conferees now, was writing a letter to her best friend Jim, inviting him to come up and spend a few days with her. Despite the storm damage and the attempted suicide and whatever other cross currents were running along beneath the surface, Orchards Cove was too beautiful a place not to share. Jim might not be potential boyfriend material, but he was a special friend and someone to talk to that she trusted. There were no restrictions that she knew of regarding overnight guests so Jim could either stay with her in her brand new palatial tent, or he could stay in one of the hotel rooms up the hill. Being the fastidious, super neat, freshly-ironed-shirt-and-polished-shoes man he was, Olympia suspected he would opt for the hotel.

This should be interesting, she thought mischievously—Jim out of his academic and ecclesiastical element. I wonder what he'd do if confronted with mama skunk and her kits. But her stream of consciousness was interrupted by the clanging of the dinner bell.

She tucked the letter into her shirt pocket and started up the hill with the rest of the folks who were staying in the campground. Her staff name tag helped with introductions, and soon she was walking along with a multi-racial family of five toward the dining hall, their dinner and the inevitable singing around the tinny old upright piano afterward. As much as Olympia didn't like singing after dinner, it was tradition, it was convivial, and it beat the hell out of an attempted suicide and being trapped on a table top in a vicious storm. Things were looking up. Poor start, good finish, she reminded herself and followed her nose to the inviting spread where, joy abounding and awaiting her arrival, there was a pitcher of vegetarian spaghetti sauce with her name on it. Life is good and getting better by the minute, she thought.

Much to everyone's relief, the first conference of the season, albeit only three days in duration, was blessedly uneventful. No storms, no health emergencies, no lost children, and everybody liked the food. On the last day all but a few attended the service in the woodland chapel and after that filled themselves to bursting with a traditional roast beef dinner complete with Yorkshire puddings, the secret surprise of the camp cook. After that, they reluctantly packed up and set off for another year.

It was Brad's custom at the end of every conference to have what he called a look-back-look forward meeting, first with the crew and then with the staff. Because the place turned around in only one day, the day was always hectic. The campsites and hotel rooms had to be ready by three in the afternoon, so Brad would hold the crew meeting right after breakfast and the staff meeting directly after lunch.

As the last of the first set of guests were packing up and leaving, Brad was thanking his staff and allowing himself a quiet sigh of satisfaction. He—no, they—had managed to pull it off. Despite all that had happened the previous week, they were up and running and would, no doubt, make it through the summer. He'd had a bit of a scramble to find a replacement for Spider, but that, too, had been sorted by the end of the first conference.

The vacancy left by Spider had been filled by a good looking young man from Boston named Norris Landrum. He was a quick study and more than happy for the work. He was also, according to the underground telephone, one hell of a guitar player. When Olympia heard that, she thought she might ask him to help out with some of her services.

Brad went on to tell them that the next group to come in would be a group of religious education professionals who came for a balanced week of church work and seaside inspiration. He went on to say these were a fun group of mostly women that were easy to work with and had a long-standing tradition of hosting a very robust and engaging happy hour. They were also known for keeping late hours ... further study, of course. He touched the side of his nose and winked.

Later he told Olympia this would likely be a light week for her because the group pretty much came with their own agenda and tended to use the resident staff more as consultants rather than workshop leaders. Even better, thought Olympia. She was thinking of the upcoming Wednesday and John Stainer and wondering how long it might take to get all of the pine needles out of her hair before then and if her one lipstick had survived the storm, and if it had, where in hell might it be hiding?

This should be interesting, she kept reminding herself. It was, after all, her first step back into the open market, so to speak, and she still didn't know whether she was buying or selling.

On Monday morning, two states apart from one another, two men were opening letters from women they cared about. Having picked up his mail, Father Jim Sawicki was finishing a second cup of coffee in the relative privacy of his office at St. Bartholomew's. Because he didn't teach summer classes at Allston College, he had more time to himself. While he often used it in personal study or expanded parish work, the letter he'd just opened offered a new and distinctly different opportunity for the use of his time. His clergy colleague and close friend, Olympia Brown, had invited him to spend some time with her in a church conference center in southern Maine. While he was no fan of tent camping, outdoor showers and mosquitoes, a week by the sea in a clean bed with meals provided, even if they were Protestant meals, was an offer he couldn't resist. She'd included the camp office phone number but suggested that he just leave a message with the best times to call and let her call him.

She told him to think about when he might like to come and for how long he might stay and included a flyer with a schedule of conferences as an FYI more than anything else. She said she didn't expect him to be particularly interested in the programs per se, other than maybe FIESTA, the gay and lesbian spirituality week offered annually by Orchards Cove, but that would be up to him and his datebook. Jim smiled.

For as long as Olympia and Jim had been friends, he didn't often bring up the subject of his personal life. Early on he'd confided to her that he was gay He knew Olympia respected his privacy and liked her all the more for it. One day he might tell her more of his story. Then again, maybe not. Either way, this was not in any way a determinant of their trust in one another or the sometimes outrageous fun they had when students or members of their congregations were out of earshot. He was already thinking what kind of wine he might bring up to share with her and, even more appealing, if they might be able to find a Michelin restaurant anywhere in the semi-immediate vicinity. Jim may have taken a vow of poverty but he still knew how to enjoy the good life when it was presented to him.

Jim smiled at the possibilities, opened his datebook and placed it on his desk. Next to it he spread out the Orchards Cove conference schedule. The third week in July was looking pretty good. If he was going on a real vacation, he would leave his clerical collar, black shoes and socks at home and bring only jeans and plaid shirts—ironed, of course. That way he might manage to look like anyone else on holiday and go undetected. One could always dream.

In the Northeast Rehab Center Spider MacCormack was having a really good day. Right after breakfast they told him he'd be released into his parents' care at the end of the week. Then later that same morning he found the letter from Paula Budreau waiting for him on his bed when he got back from his morning group therapy session. That she wrote at all was more than he could have hoped for, and that she wanted to see him was even better. Even the camp chaplain, Olympia Brown, had asked for him. No wonder he felt great.

He was more in charge of his life than he had been for a long time. He was learning so much, learning and planning for the days and weeks ahead. Spider was beginning have a plan, and connecting with Paula was part of it. As long as he walked the walk, talked the talk and convinced everyone he really was stable and in good health, there would be a pretty good chance he could pull it off. Spider refolded the letter and tucked it under his pillow. It was time to go down to the exercise room and work out. He needed to be in control of his body as well as his mind.

Later in the afternoon, when they had free time, he'd write back to Paula. Then he wondered how long it might be before he would be allowed to drive. Stay in the moment, he told himself as he walked toward the exercise room. First, you answer the letter, and then you wait to see what she says.

By Tuesday Olympia knew that Brad Davies had been right on the mark when he'd told her this would be an easy week. The RE people, as they referred to themselves, had planned their week to the hilt. They were cheery, pleasant and totally focused, and also as predicted, they played just as hard as they worked. Courtesy of their abundant hospitality, Olympia never once opened one of her own bottles of wine and skipped more than one meal because she was over-full of chips, cheese and homemade salsa.

However, underneath the bon-bons and bonhomie of this week's conference, two recurrent thoughts kept poking little holes in her inner calm. The first and more immediate was her Wednesday lunch date with John Stainer, and the other was Spider MacCormack. She had some measure of control over the first one, and while admitting to being a bit nervous, she was really looking forward to it. The second, Spider, was completely out of her control but nonetheless continued to be a concern. As a chaplain she could justify a visit or a thinking-of-you card but nothing more. No, cancel that. She decided that other than the greeting she'd already sent through Paula, any further contact would have to be initiated by him. With that more or less settled in her mind, she turned her thoughts to, yikes, tomorrow. Less than twenty-four hours from now, she was going out on a real live date!

Fourteen

On Wednesday morning fifty-year-old Olympia Brown was positively girlish. She fished what passed for a mirror out of her toiletries bag and surveyed the playing field. She took out the lipstick and travel bottle of mouthwash and put them into her handbag. No perfume; it made her sneeze.

Next were the clothes: preaching pants, light ones, and flowered top, long purple and green one. Earrings, Indian beaded ones, the silver chalice necklace that was the symbol of her denomination, and finally white multi-strap sandals. Wipe them down, and hope for the best.

By eleven she was done and dusted and as ready as she ever would be. So with nothing else to procrastinate with, she pulled her beloved VW van out of the parking area and turned north, sure that every butterfly in southern Maine had taken up residence in her stomach. I started this, she told herself as she hung onto the steering wheel for dear life, and I'm damn well going to see it through. If he's a total jerk, I never have to see him again, and if I get nervous and act like a total jerk, he'll never have to see me again. Oh, crap, what if he chickens out? What if he stands me up? That bastard! Thus, the Reverend Doctor Olympia Brown, Summer Chaplain at Orchards Cove Religious Conference Center, lurched and seesawed to the South Portland exit off Route 95 and the Gourmet Burger, Fifty Kinds of Burgers and All the Fixings, parking lot.

"Damn," she said aloud. "I never asked what kind of car he drives."

She found a space near the exit sign and then did a final check in the visor mirror. Having forgotten to bring a comb, she finger-brushed her short hair into place. Then she ran her tongue over her teeth, shot up with a squirt of the breath spray and declared herself ready for battle. She was, as planned, fifteen minutes early. This would give her the advantage of the first sighting.

Once inside the restaurant she was assailed by the heavenly scents of frying onions, garlic—and charcoal broiled cow. Shrugging off her vegetarian distaste, she did a quick look-around but did not see anyone wearing a Hawaiian shirt. So far, so good. She asked the hostess for a table for two by a window, if that was possible. It was. There she settled in facing the door, asked for a glass of water and a cup of black coffee and pulled out the ratty looking paperback she kept for times like this. Then she saw him, blisteringly yellow and lime green and fuchsia flowered shirt and all, coming from the direction of the bathrooms, making straight for her table. Subtle, he wasn't.

"Reverend Olympia?"

"Oh, please, John, its Olympia. The Reverend part is mostly reserved for Sundays."

He pulled out a chair. "Ollie, then?" He sat.

She smiled over her clenched teeth and said, "Nope, no nicknames, least of all that one. I've always been Olympia."

He held out his hand over the plates and napkins. "Hello, Olympia. I'm John Stainer. Thank you for coming." He paused and added, "I was afraid you might not show up."

Olympia smiled for real this time. "I had the same thought driving up here. I'm wicked out of practice at this sort of thing."

"But you're a born New Englander, that's for sure."

"How can you tell?"

"Let's just say I'm wicked sure."

'Oh,' she said, this time with a real smile. "Caught me out, didn't you?"

"Takes one to know one. I grew up in Somerville, Massachusetts, but came up here to college and never left."

"What do you do?"

"Mmm, a little of this and a little of that."

"What this and what that? You said you owned your own business."

"Let's order first, and then I'll tell you, but then it's your turn. Looks like the waitperson is heading in our direction. What perfect timing."

The young man, wearing black knee-length shorts and a beige Gourmet Burger logo tee-shirt, appeared, carrying Olympia's water and coffee and two oversized laminated menus. Minutes later, Olympia announced her vegetarianism and ordered a grilled vegetable and goat cheese burrito. John asked if she minded if he ordered a burger, and when she said she did not, he returned to perusing the menu. The choices were legion and daunting.

Olympia used the opportunity to look the man over. He was decidedly more than middling weight but not obese. She couldn't really guess his height. Sitting across from one another, they were more or less eye-level, but he'd come in for a landing so quickly when he arrived that she was unable to make any sort of guess. Size did not matter to Olympia. Personality, mental acuity and a person's value system would be what determined her interest for yay or for nay. Right now, John was still in neutral waters. His shirt was outrageous but said something about him. The man had a big personality.

Her own choice of the long, flowing blouse and sandals made a statement which said middle-aged hippie wannabe. John ordered a gorgonzola cheese and green apple hamburger, and asked if she'd like a beer or a glass of wine with her lunch. When she declined, he did, as well, and suggested perhaps another time. Olympia smiled and sipped her coffee.

The place was busy, and the service was quick. John was not long into explaining to Olympia that he was self-employed as a woodworker and furniture refinisher and the owner of a small antique and vintage curio shop in Newcastle, a little coastal town next to Damariscotta.

Olympia snapped to attention. In her secret life she was a yard sale and secondhand store junkie and was immediately interested in knowing more about something they might have in common. John was only too pleased to oblige. By the time their heaping plates arrived they were chatting away. He was so easy to talk to, and Olympia wondered why she'd ever been nervous about meeting him.

They took their time eating, asking and answering questions about one another, and eventually setting down their cutlery as a sign that they were finished. Almost immediately the waiter came and cleared away their plates. As he did so Olympia glanced discreetly at her watch and was astounded to see it was already two o'clock.

The young man returned with the dessert menu, which she waved away after ordering a second coffee. John ordered the house specialty, apple pie with two scoops of ice cream and an extra spoon. Was I that obvious, she thought, or is he being the teensiest bit presumptive? She did, however, insist on paying her own bill.

By three o'clock they'd told each other as much as they wanted to in a first meeting and agreed to meet again. Now they were standing in the sun-warmed parking lot, talking about where and when that might be.

"Wednesdays are usually good for me," said Olympia, squinting at him. She had forgotten her sunglasses and was shading her light green eyes against the sun.

"That's great, and daytimes are best for me too. I like to keep the shop open in the evening during the tourist season. It's next to a restaurant, and I get quite a few walk-ins while they are waiting for their tables."

"You never told me the name of your shop."

"The Down-Mainah," he said and spelled it out. "It's on Main Street, a fun play on words. So how about lunch again next Wednesday? Maybe this time you'll let me buy you a glass of wine."

"I'll think about that," she said.

"If you don't mind, I'd rather you called me at the number I gave you. You said you were hard to reach, and most evenings I'm holed up in there. It's the shop number. How about Sunday? I'll be there all afternoon."

Olympia agreed, and the two parted company, but not before John thanked Olympia for coming and gave her a quick kiss on the cheek. Olympia tooted and waved as she pulled out of the parking lot and grinned all the way back to Orchards Cove.

When she got back there was a pink slip message in her mail box. "Please call Jim around supper time at the rectory." There was no number, but that was Jim being extra careful. He knew she'd memorized his various numbers long ago. I have time for a quick late afternoon swim, she thought. It's a beautiful day, and I haven't really spent any time on the beach yet.

This required a trek back to her tent to check on the cats, change into her swim suit and loop an aluminum chair and her beachbag over her arm. The day was glorious. The vile humidity of the week before was history, and the conferees and many of the crew were out in force, taking advantage of it.

The beach itself was the stuff of Chamber of Commerce postcards. Light beige sand, sparkling blue water, slow rolling waves and a rainbow of people in beach attire scattered along the shore. The sand was warm but not so hot that you couldn't walk on it. Olympia looked around and spied an artist couple she'd met earlier in the week, Maxine and Henry. She'd already forgotten their last names. She padded across the soft sand and asked if she could join them. The two simultaneously bid her welcome, and Olympia opened her chair and settled herself beside them.

"Have you been in the water yet?" asked Olympia

Maxine, the chattier of the two, responded. "Are you kidding, woman? You are in Maine. On a good day the water temperature is 55 degrees, and on a positively tropical day it's 57. Besides which, there's usually a wicked undertow and sudden drop-offs that change location with every storm. Only kids and dogs go in the water up here, and that's with a lifeguard right behind them. Nope, not me. I like to walk along the edge at low tide and look for sea glass, but nothing above the knees for this woman."

Henry nodded agreement, and Olympia, thinking them both to be weak and self-indulgent, pondered this in her heart but said nothing. She was a born and bred New Englander. She'd been swimming in these waters since she was born. She'd show them how real women took on the sea in New England. She got up, dropped her towel on her chair and started down the sandy incline toward the water's edge.

"Don't say I didn't warn you," Maxine called after her.

Olympia harrumphed under her breath and then stomped her right foot into the shallow water and gasped but refused to scream. Too proud to admit defeat and turn back, she walked resolutely forward until the freezing water was above her knees and then, gritting her teeth, dived into an oncoming wave. "Holy shit," was all she could gasp when she surfaced and was grateful there was no one nearby to hear her. Then, wasting no time at all, she scrabbled through the soft sand and pebbles under the shallows and galloped back to the warmth and safety of her chair.

"How was it?" asked Maxine."

"Refreshing," said Olympia.

"Liar," said Maxine and tossed her a second towel.

By the time her teeth stopped chattering, it was time to go back and get dressed for dinner and make that call to Jim.

Fifteen

Olympia didn't fully warm up after her bravado plunge into stupidity until that evening when she was double wrapped in sweaters and zipped tightly into her sleeping bag, but two hours later she was standing stark naked in her tent, covered in sweat and tossing off the all the layers in favor of a dry sheet and nothing else. This had been happening more and more of late. One minute she'd be freezing, and the next, boiling. She knew full well what was causing this and took it as another indicator that she needed more than a biological change in her life. The clock was ticking.

After she'd dried off and cooled down, she got back into bed and thought about the day or, more specifically, John Stainer. Was he a person of interest? Too soon to tell. He certainly talked a good line, but was it a line or the real thing? Certainly worth a second look, and since that was in the works, her thoughts moved on to her phone conversation with Jim. He was actually going to come up, and better yet, for a whole week. She was thrilled. He would stay in the hotel. She was not surprised. They would go out to dinner. She expected that. He suggested that on her day off they might go down to Ogunquit and walk the Marginal Way along the craggy cliff. She didn't question that.

She did not mention John Stainer but rather decided to wait until she'd had a second date with him before forming any sort of opinion that she might be willing to share with Jim. The truth was she was still getting used to the idea that going out on a date could lead to lead to something more. The question remained, was she ready for this?

By now her body temperature had stabilized, and sleep was overtaking her. She gave in gratefully as she listened to the familiar grunts and scrabblings of the creatures who nightly visited her campsite. She loved hearing those sounds and slowly drifted down into sleep, content and smiling.

Spider MacCormack was not drifting into sleep. In fact, it was just the opposite. He'd been secretly cutting back on his meds so he wouldn't feel quite so groggy and lethargic, especially in the morning. At night he occupied his racing thoughts with plans for when he was out of the hospital. There were two threads spinning through his thinking. One, not surprisingly, was Paula Budreau. She'd written to him right after she'd gotten his first message, and he'd written right back, saying he'd let her know as soon as he was out. In his response he asked her to promise not to mention the fact that they were still in touch to anyone. He knew she'd spoken to Olympia Brown and was sure she could be trusted, but no one else. Besides, to all appearances it was a romantic interest, and for now anyway, that was a good thing.

The second, much more tangled, thread was Derek Jamison. Paula was his unsuspecting connection to Derek. As long as he was careful he could keep tabs on Derek's actions and whereabouts with no one the wiser. Spider knew how to be careful. He'd spent the better part of his life trying to stay beneath the radar. So why would he behave any differently now? It's what people were used to, and Spider was counting on that.

The rest of Olympia's week was a pleasant mix of camp chaplain duties, companionable after-hours staff gatherings and personal time on the beach. Add to this, much to her own surprise and amazement, she was actually beginning to enjoy the ritual singing after supper. This had improved exponentially when the new kid on the block, Norris, joined in with his guitar and extraordinary voice. While she would always feel bad for Spider and what had happened to him, watching and listening to Norris was better than having seconds on dessert. Well, almost. That guy could sing.

Saturday night for many of the conferences was banquet and talent show night. Usually it was a fish fry for dinner, but if people wanted to pay extra, they could have lobster. Olympia shuddered at the thought of it, but what else do non-vegetarians eat in Maine? She usually skipped the meal entirely and used the time to work on her sermon and get ready for the worship service the next morning.

This particular evening she felt sufficiently prepared to go up the hill and enjoy the talent show. It was predictably a mishmashed combination of everything from lisping three-year-olds reciting "Mary Had a Little Lamb" to one of the crew kids playing a Bach violin sonata. All were given rapt attention and duly applauded when they took their bows. Olympia was so caught up in the whole thing that she didn't notice Paula Budreau slip in beside her. It was only when Paula tapped her on the arm and whispered something that she realized who it was.

"Would you mind repeating that? I didn't really hear you," whispered Olympia.

Paula leaned closer. "I got another letter from Spider today. Have you got a minute?"

Olympia held up her finger and waited until the next round of applause before slipping out of her seat and following Paula outside. The two walked out onto one of the paths that crisscrossed the campus until they came to a wooden bench. Olympia could still hear the sounds of laughter and clapping, but for all intents and purposes she and Paula were alone.

"Spider got out of the hospital yesterday. He called and left a message. Of course he didn't leave his name, just a number. He wants to see me."

"How do you feel about that?" asked Olympia.

"I don't know. I would like to see him, but I guess I'm nervous. Like, is he OK, or is he still … jeez, I don't know how to say it."

"Troubled?" offered Olympia.

"Yeah."

Olympia considered her words carefully. The decision was Paula's, but she had asked for guidance. "As I remember, you have a car. You could offer to visit him at his parents' home. That way you wouldn't be alone with him if you didn't want to, and you could see for yourself how he is."

Paula sat up straighter. "Gee, that's a great idea. Since he gave me a number to call, I can talk to him a couple of times first so I can see how he is. Then I could go down there if I wanted to. He lives in Portsmouth, so it's not too far."

Perfect, thought Olympia. It was clear that Paula was testing the waters herself. Spider was a very troubled young man, and such people can latch onto others in hopes of distracting themselves from their own issues. A few telephone conversations, followed by what would, in fact, be a supervised visit, sounded like a perfect way forward.

"Good thinking," said Olympia. "Take it one day at a time. He's had a rough go of it, and it's not going to be an easy comeback."

"Oh, I forgot to tell you, he says hi, and thank you again for all you did that night. He said he doesn't mind you knowing he's writing to me, but would rather the rest of the people up here didn't."

"I can understand that," said Olympia, "and let me know how it goes, OK? That is, if you want to."

Paula laughed, clearly feeling more relaxed now.

"I don't think there'll be much to tell. He's pretty quiet, you know, or at least he was. Remember, I really don't know him very well."

Olympia did not bother to tell her that her mother used to say, "Watch out for the quiet ones." She was pretty sure it would have fallen on deaf ears.

On his second night home Spider was sitting with his parents, watching TV, and if he was bored senseless he didn't let it show. Above all was keeping up the appearance of good health and mental stability so he could start going out on his own again. As he stared at the kaleidoscope of flickering images on the screen in front of him, in his mind he was elsewhere, planning the details of his first visit with Paula. Of course she would have to come to his house. That way, everyone would see how well he was doing, and the sooner he'd get out from under his parents' anxious twenty-four/seven scrutiny. He crossed his arms behind his head and leaned back against the sofa. Spider MacCormack was the very picture of relaxation and well-being.

Like Olympia, Father Jim was getting ready for his own kind of Sunday. This would be the celebrations of the three Sunday Masses at St. Bartholomew's and visiting the ill and elderly after that. His Saturday night routine was always the same: a warmed-up supper of whatever the housekeeper had cooked for him on Friday, then prayer and study on the text for the next day, and then a glass of good wine along with the eleven o'clock news. It was comfortable, predictable—and lonely. This is what he had chosen for himself, and by and large he was satisfied with his life, but for reasons he chose not to dwell upon, Saturday nights were hard. He tried not to let his thoughts drift back to those happier Saturday nights, but on some days that simply wasn't possible. On those nights he would have a second glass of wine.

Tonight wasn't one of those nights, but he was very aware of how nice it was going to be to get completely away from everything familiar and be incognito for an entire week. He smiled and sipped at his wine, a full-bodied Bordeaux, and began counting his blessings. First on the list was Olympia Brown.

Derek was sitting alone on the beach. It was dark, and everyone else was at the talent show. When the wind was right he could hear wisps of music and soft bursts of applause, but he wasn't listening. Derek was trying to figure out Norris Landrum. The guy had been an instant hit the day he arrived. He was easy to talk to, a good—no, a fantastic—musician, and as strong as an ox. There was no job on campus that was too dirty or tough for him, and he did what was asked of him with good humor and an easy smile. So what was it that was getting under Derek's skin?

Derek was never going to admit, even to himself, alone in the dark on the beach, that he was jealous of the young man's personality, talent or good looks. But the more he stewed over it, he finally began to realize what it was. Norris did precisely what he wanted to do in precisely his own time without ever actually confronting Derek or challenging his authority. But how did he do it, and more importantly, how could Derek deal with it? How do you pin down a guy you can't pin down? Derek needed to be in charge of his team. He was being paid to be the crew boss and expected things to go his way. It wasn't that Norris did anything wrong or bad, he just wasn't asking, "How high?" when Derek said, "Jump."

The fact that Norris was black didn't help either. One wrong look or word, and Derek would be labeled a racist. He stood and brushed the sand off his legs and backside. There was more than one way to skin a cat. He just needed to find out what it was.

At nine-thirty John Stainer turned off the lights, locked the door of The Down-Mainah and walked down the street and around the corner to the local watering hole for his nightly beer. The Pint and Pickle was an English pub knockoff that was favored by the locals and mercifully overlooked by the tourists. It was dark, smoky and smelled of spilled beer and French fries. Here is where the townies gathered to go over the gossip of the day, tell a few well-worn off-color jokes and complain about the tourists whose custom they all depended upon. It was the kind of place where everybody knew everybody else, and if you missed more than two nights in a row, somebody went out to find you.

John was almost halfway through his beer when Perley Yettin, his best friend since childhood, remarked on how quiet he was and asked if anything was the matter.

"Just thinking about the weather," said John. "I hear that storm they had down south last week was real bad. I'm going down to Portland next week and was just wondering what's predicted."

"Ayuh," said Perley, looking at Stainer over his beer. "Weathah's weathah. It comes, it goes, just like the tourists." He was a man of few words.

Sixteen

It was Sunday, and Spider MacCormack had been out of the hospital for three days. He was eating huge portions of his over-anxious mother's home cooking, sleeping in his own bed and walking the dog at least twice a day and more often if the dog was up to it. He was doing his best to pick up the pieces of the life that had been scattered from here to hell and back the night he jumped off the dresser at Orchards Cove. However, under the calm exterior he presented to the world, he feared nothing would ever be the same or normal again. He knew his parents meant well, but in fact, they were more hindrance than help. Since he'd returned one or the other of them was always around, either right there or in the next room. About the only time he could be truly alone was in the bathroom, and how many times a day can a guy pee or take a shower or walk the dog?

He knew they were freaked out by what had happened, but so was he. He knew damn well what sent him over the edge that night, and there wasn't a soul in the world he'd ever tell. He would, however, bide his time, make his plans, and one day go back there and get even. He wasn't telling anybody that either.

Spider got up off the sofa started jogging in place. Intense activity helped to push back the ugly thoughts that still threatened to undo him. It was important to stay positive. Exercise helped with that. That was one of the things he'd learned when he was in the hospital. The other was to keep your thoughts to yourself.

He jumped up and down, flapped his arms, took a few deep breaths and reminded himself that today was a good day. He'd had a call from Paula Budreau, and she'd agreed to come and visit on her next day off. Now all he needed to do was to convince his parents to let them walk into town for ice cream or a pizza by themselves. If worse came to worst, he'd offer to take the dog along as a chaperone.

At Orchards Cove it was all hands on deck. Sunday was changeover day. The RE conference was over, and families were already arriving with their offspring for the Youth Leadership Development Week. According to local gossip, this was the noisiest, least organized and most fun of any week up there. On a good day, working with teens was not unlike herding cats; but take them away from home and parental supervision, feed them well and then turn them loose in the woods and by the sea, and it was an experience like no other. Brad Davies gave the senior staff a quick overview and warning of what they might expect.

Nurse Ellie was a seasoned staff member and was there to back him up. Olympia had worked with church kids before and really enjoyed the challenge and the surprises that bright, articulate and sometimes impetuous teenagers could bring to a day. She was psyched and ready to go.

In a more cautious tone, Brad told them that because the conferees were so close in age to the crew, situations, as he delicately put it, had developed in the past that needed attention.

"Just keep your eyes and ears open and let me know if there is anything that might bear watching. For some of these kids, it's their first time away from home, and it can be a little overwhelming."

Olympia nodded in understanding. Brad didn't need to say any more. It was not unlike parenting. With teens there always needed to be a delicate balance between respecting their growing independence and letting them go completely unsupervised. Sometimes you got it right, and sometimes you didn't. Paying attention was the best anyone could do.

Olympia knew she was good at being attentive. As a minister and college professor, it was her stock in trade. Her mind wandered. Yes, listening, teaching and preaching was what she did, but it was beginning to lose its edge. Or was it she who was losing her edge? How could she know for sure, and then what?

"Olympia?"

"Mmmph?" Olympia blinked herself back into the present.

"I just asked if you had anything special you might do with the kids for tonight's evensong?"

"Sorry, Brad, my brain just took a little side trip. I have thought about it, and I'm planning to ask Norris if he might help out. He's so much closer to their age and music than I am. I thought it might be a good entry point. Music and telling their own stories has always worked well for this age group."

"I like it," said Brad. Then he went over more scheduling details. There were always a few changes from conference to conference. Wake-up and breakfast were always an hour later for teen week, and banquet night, rather than lobster, which none of them could afford, was all-you-can-eat pizza followed by make-your-own ice cream sundaes.

By now Olympia was all ears. Teen week was sounding better and better, especially the pizza and ice cream part. It was a good thing Jim, gourmet food and wine snob that he was, was coming the following week. He might just faint dead away if forced to eat both at the same sitting.

Dragging herself back into the present for a second time, she listened to Brad adjourn the meeting and wish them well for the upcoming week. She turned to leave and saw Ellie, the camp nurse, waving at her.

"I could use some time off for good behavior. You want to bug off and go have lunch somewhere off campus?" she asked?

"Sounds good. Where did you have in mind?"

"All that talk about pizza and ice cream made me hungry. There's a great little burger and pizza place about two miles from here."

"I have a better idea," said Olympia with broad smile. "Let's just skip the pizza and go straight for the ice cream."

Ellie did not need convincing.

At four in the afternoon, still feeling the after-effects of too much ice cream, Olympia dialed the number John Stainer had given her last week.

"Down-Mainah," said a voice she now recognized.

"Hi, John, its Olympia. Are we still on for lunch this week?"

"I am if you am," he said with a chuckle.

Olympia rolled her eyes. "Where shall we meet then? You know the area better than I do."

"You like Thai?"

Olympia loved Thai food and told him so.

"Well, there's the Thai Won On in Portland's Old Port area. That's the old part of the city. Food's great there. We can walk around the waterfront afterward, if you like. It's real pretty and historical, too."

Olympia agreed, wrote down the address and phone number of the place and ended with, "See you soon."

On the way back to her tent, she took note of the fact that this felt like more of a chore than a date, something to be done and then crossed off the list. Oh, well, she'd give him a second chance, and this Wednesday was it.

All Sunday long and starting right after breakfast, Derek and the crew were flat out. Tent sites had to be picked up, hotel rooms changed over, and conferees, both leaving and arriving, needed assistance with packing, parking and taking down and setting up tents. It was always chaotic, and Derek's worst day of the week. He liked law and order and things in their proper places, and Sundays didn't come close. The best he could do was keep an even temper as he galloped from site to site, checking on each of the work groups, making sure they were on target and checking if they needed anything. At the very end of the day, after the staff introductions and orientation ritual, he had his own tradition.

At his suggestion, and with Brad's approval and funding, he ordered in buckets of fried clams, French fries, onion rings and a case of beer for the crew. This was the time each week when he thanked them for all their hard work and reminded them to keep it up. But, never one to let a moment pass him by that he couldn't work to his own advantage, Derek also used the party time to observe—spy, actually—on the group and see who was hanging out with whom. He moved among them, stopping here and there to chomp down another clam or a fist full of fries and say a few words. If some of them went silent when he approached, he pretended not to notice. He had a job to do.

The one thing that continued to worry him, which he kept to himself, was the whole thing with Spider. He wondered if Spider had said anything to anyone. There had been an incident, but as far as he knew, nobody knew of it. If they do ask me, I'll just deny it, he told himself. I mean, the guy was nuts, right? No one in his right mind tries to kill himself, right? That's proof enough, he'd tell them if they asked, and he hoped no one would. Out of the corner of his eye he saw Norris, Paula and Miguel Dos Santos sitting together on the sofa, chatting and laughing among themselves.

Derek moved to the center of the room and blew out a piercing whistle.

"OK, guys, we're out of food and beer, so it's time to call it a night. We've got an early call tomorrow. The teens want to build a sweat lodge down in the campground, and we have to get them the branches and stuff."

There was a communal groan.

He held up his hands in mock innocence. "Hey, look, I don't write the orders, I just carry them out."

This was followed by a general good-natured rumbling as all but two drifted off to their rooms. Norris Landrum and Paula Budreau decided to go out for a walk.

The two walked along, each soon matching the other's stride and rhythm, and after a turn around the upper campus, decided to go down onto the beach. There was enough of a moon so that finding their way wasn't a problem. The soft, sea-washed quietness of the night was a treat after the noisy chaos of the day. They chatted about where they were going to school. He was studying science and engineering at Northeastern University in Boston, and she was a graphic arts major at Pratt. They talked about the Orchards Cove experience, whatever that was, and eventually about the crew and their diverse personalities—in other words, local gossip.

They quickly discovered they both liked almost everyone they worked with but shared a general discomfort in Derek's presence. Paula wondered if Norris knew anything about what had happened to Spider, and if not, if she should say anything. She'd promised Spider not to talk about their being in contact now, but that didn't include what happened before the accident, and it was the very reason Norris was here beside her in more ways than one, she thought with an uncomfortable shiver.

"You cold?" asked Norris.

"Hardly, it's beautiful out. No, I was just thinking of the person whose spot you filled."

"Oh, you mean Spider Somebody-or-other, the one who tried to hang himself with a sheet."

"That's the one." She was about to add that she'd been friends with him but caught herself just in time.

"He was a nice kid, I liked him. I can only hope he'll be OK. We all sent him a card after it happened."

"The guys told me about it when I first got here. It must have been awful."

"Worse than awful. I think we all felt a little guilty, like we maybe we could have done something to help him. Anyway, it's over. They took him to the hospital, and the next day Brad went to see him and told us he's going to get better."

"Poor guy," was all Norris said.

"Uh huh." Paula covered a huge yawn and said she needed to get back and go to bed.

The two walked back to the wooden boardwalk, collected their shoes and dusted the sand off their feet and ankles. Barefoot and thoughtful, they padded softly down the path and back to the crew shack. When they reached the door Norris paused and began to speak.

"You know, I'm glad I got the job and everything, but I have to say it feels kind of creepy to be taking the place of a guy who tried to kill himself."

"I don't know what to tell you. I knew him a little bit—well enough to know there was something bothering him, but no more than that. He wasn't much of a talker. Anyway, he's getting help, and there's nothing more we can do. You shouldn't let it bother you. I'm glad you've come."

"I suppose," said Norris, "it's just …"

Paula smacked him playfully on the shoulder. "Lighten up. This place is great. Derek can be pushy, but he's just doing his job. I think it all goes to his head sometimes. Just keep your head down and look busy. That's what I do. You know what my favorite tee-shirt says, don't you?"

"No. What?"

"Jesus is coming, look busy."

He laughed and added, "I saw another one that says, Jesus is coming, and boy is he pissed!"

The two of them were laughing when Norris reached out and put his hands on Paula's shoulder.

"Goodnight, Paula. Thanks for coming out with me. It was fun."

"Good night yourself. See you in the morning."

The two parted in the dim hallway outside the common room. Neither of them saw Derek Jamison sitting in the dark, taking in every word.

Seventeen

By ten o'clock on Monday morning, Orchards Cove was literally buzzing with activity. Most of the crew members were engaged in dragging and stacking branches in the center of the camp circle. The real buzzing sound was provided by a chain-saw wielding Derek, who was masterfully cutting and trimming the remaining storm broken branches as directed. To the uninitiated observer, it was good-natured, noisy chaos. In reality it was a carefully crafted exercise in leadership and collaborative decision-making along with team-building and development of community.

With the support of their adult advisors, the teens needed to choose who would direct the activity, who would design and actually construct the lodge and finally designate a program team, which would determine and design the rituals and activities which would take place within the structure itself. Olympia thought the whole idea was brilliant, but if she was looking for some quiet time with her cats on a Monday morning, the campground was not the place.

On the other hand, was she really in desperate need of quiet, she asked herself? The answer was an emphatic no. The sounds were happy ones, the day was beautiful, warmer than the day before, but not humid, and with a second, or was it her third, cup of coffee on the ground beside her, she couldn't ask for anything more.

Paula Budreau used the noise and the activity as a way to slip out of the work team unnoticed and see if Olympia was at home and alone. With all the whoozing and crunching,

Olympia didn't hear Paula's approach, but when she looked up to see her walking down the path, she waved a happy greeting. Then she noticed Paula's frown and troubled expression and wondered what might be the problem.

"Hi, Olympia, do you have a minute? Something happened this morning, and I haven't a clue what to do about it. I don't have much time because I'm supposed to be helping out over there." She gestured to where most of the noise was coming from.

"Sure, Paula. Sit down and tell me."

"Last night after the orientation, I went for a walk with Norris, you know, the new guy. It was no big deal. We just didn't feel like going to bed, so we went out for a while. I mean, it was hardly a date or anything, right?"

"Sounds pretty casual to me," said Olympia, wondering what could possibly be coming next.

"Well, this morning, I was walking to breakfast, and Derek comes up behind me and kind of grabs onto my arm, not hard or anything, just grabs on and tells me that it's not a good idea to go walking alone on the beach with people I don't know. Can you believe that?"

Olympia flinched and hoped Paula didn't see it. She didn't like what she was hearing, but given what she was beginning to know about Derek, she wasn't all that surprised. Maybe it was because he had his eye set on Paula for himself, or maybe it was more than that. "Did he say anything else?"

Paula nodded. "He said he'd overheard our conversation, mine and Norris's, when we came in from our walk." She paused and pushed a strand of hair behind her ear. "Well, we were talking about Derek, and we did say he was kind of pushy, but that's all. I have to say I wish he hadn't heard it. Now I'm going to be on his bad side, and that's one of the things Spider told me, not to get on his bad side. You remember me telling you that?"

Olympia nodded. Paula certainly didn't lack for sheer volume of words. "So how can I help you?"

"I don't know. I just know I needed to tell you, mostly because the last thing Derek said to me was, 'Go have your breakfast, and don't ever say anything about what I just told you, because I'll deny it.'"

Olympia blew out a long breath and slowly moved her head from side to side. "That, plain and simple, is a threat, Paula."

"I thought so, but who'd believe me, and what do I do now?"

"Telling me was the first and best thing you could have done. Now go write it down. In other words, keep a written and dated record of anything he does that is in any way disturbing or upsetting to you. Keep an eye on him. He sounds like a bully, and bullies depend on fear and secrecy for their control. They're often sneaky, just like this morning. You know, no witnesses. They make people fear them and afraid to talk about what is happening because it might get worse, and it usually does. That's how they control people."

"I have to tell you, he really made me nervous. Don't ask me why, but now I'm thinking about Spider. Do you suppose Derek was bullying him? I know he never missed a chance to pick on him or make fun of him. He was sneaky about that, too. The only reason I know is because I asked Spider about it."

"What did he say?"

"Like I said before, he told me not to get on Derek's bad side. Hey, look, Olympia, I have to get back, but thanks for this. I'll do what you said, and if anything else happens I'll write it down."

"Do that, Paula, but for God's sake keep whatever you write in a safe place. The last thing you want is for someone else to find it. Another thing, and this is just my thinking, but I need to say it. You can walk on the beach with anyone you want. I'm glad you told me all of this, and it goes without saying that I'll keep it in confidence."

With that Paula thanked her and sprinted off, looking for all the world like a young, tanned, healthy gazelle full of life and energy and the joy of living. Olympia sat and watched her disappear down the path. "Take care of yourself, Kiddo," she whispered.

When she did find a quiet time and she would not be interrupted, Olympia would think long and hard on what Paula said that morning. She knew Paula was planning to go and see Spider on Wednesday, and it might be good to arrange a check-in with her after that. Olympia was unconsciously drumming her fingers on the aluminum arm of her chair. She did that when she was thinking, or more likely, plotting. It just so happened she was planning to meet with Norris that very afternoon to work out some of the music for the nightly evensongs. It might be the perfect time to find out firsthand what he thought of the Orchards Cove experience.

Off to the side of the swirling construction project, Brad was standing with his arms crossed, watching the unsteady progress. Once the lodge was completed he'd crawl inside and do a quick safety check. Fire and safety regulations required any number of modifications from what would have been an authentic Native American model, not the least of which was the size and nature of the fire allowed inside. This had to be small, covered with a fire screen and there must be several buckets of water and portable fire extinguishers within five feet of the flame. Not at all unreasonable, the teens agreed and added these to the to-do list. This is how it's supposed to be, he thought, bright young people working and learning together and having a good time doing it. Maybe, finally, things were getting back to normal.

It would take generations to grow back the trees which had been destroyed, but considering no lives had been lost, not even Spider's, Brad was beginning to relax. Each season came with its own internal drama, but this one took the cake as far as he was concerned. Now, as he watched the kids buzzing with excitement and with the weather forecast favorable for the rest of the week, he might even allow himself the afternoon off.

It was Paula who broke into the daydream and invited him to inspect their work.

Later, as he was leaving the campground to go back to his office, he saw Derek and Norris sitting together at one of the picnic tables. That's good, he thought, they're here to help if needed but not obvious about it, just the way it should be.

Only it wasn't just as it should be. Derek and Norris were having a low-pitched, high-tension conversation. Derek was speaking.

"I don't know what you're talkin' about, man. I divide up the work as I get it. First come, first served. I don't hear anyone else complaining, so what's your problem?"

"Seems like shit-house duty always falls my way, Derek. If you don't mind, I'd like something else once in a while. Something a little less, uh, hands on. I've been keeping track, and I got it every day last week and now every day this week, so far anyway."

"Work's work, Norris. It's got to be done. I can't help it if you keep pulling the short straw. The smell bother you? I'd think you'd be used to it by now."

Norris clenched both fists under the table but refused to rise to the bait. He was better than this, and he knew it even if Derek didn't. "I'm suggesting we put up a chart with the jobs that need to be done every day and then just rotate our way through it. That way everybody gets a chance to do the easy ones and the not-so-easy ones. Anything wrong with that?"

"I don't like it, that's what's wrong with it."

"You mean you didn't think of it, is what's wrong with it."

Derek's neck and cheeks flushed a dark red. He pointed a finger at Derek.

"Look, boy…"

Norris leaned forward, took a very tight hold of Derek's wrist and looked him straight in the eye.

"Don't ever call me boy," was all he said.

Around four in the afternoon Olympia went up the hill in search of Norris. She had a sheaf of song sheets under her arm and was eager to enlist him to be part of her evening programs. The terms evensong and vespers had their linguistic roots and practices in medieval monasticism. Today they were enjoying a renaissance as people today looked for new, less ritualistic, ways to express their sense and feeling of the spiritual. The idea of gathering together for quiet music and meditation at the end of a day was gaining popularity in situations and communities like Orchards Cove. It was not exactly church, but it was reverential, and it was, for lack of a better term, worshipful. It made for a gentle ending of the day.

Norris was sitting on one of the wooden benches, watching some of the littler kids playing on the swings and monkey bars. She approached and asked if she might join him. He smiled, waved her toward him and turned in her direction.

"Good afternoon, Reverend Chaplain."

"Hi, Norris. I know I mentioned it before, but now I'm asking you for real. Will you be willing to help out with music at some of the evening programs this week? I've heard you and watched how the kids respond after supper. I think it would be perfect for what I have in mind."

Norris ducked his head and smiled. "I'd be honored, Ma'am. Just tell me what you'd like and when you'd like me to do it."

For the next few minutes they worked out the details of what Olympia had in mind. He had a few ideas and suggestions himself, and between the two of them, they had a plan in very short order.

Olympia gathered up her papers and turned again to Norris.

"I hope you don't mind my asking, but I was wondering how it's going? You really didn't have the orientation that the others had."

He looked puzzled.

"You came up here because we had an emergency situation, and you had to hit the deck running, as they say."

"Oh, you mean the kid who tried to hang himself."

Olympia gulped. "In a word, yes."

"Funny, Paula Budreau asked me the same question last night while we were out for a walk. Why is everybody so concerned about me all of a sudden?"

Olympia said nothing about what she knew of the previous night's conversation, but only, "Human and professional interest. You came up here in a shower of sparks, so to speak, not the easiest way to start a new job. It was kind of an odd vacancy to have to fill. Some people might feel a little freaked out by it. Just checking. Maybe it's a chaplain thing."

Norris gave her an odd look and said, "Funny you should ask."

"Why?"

He looked to the left and right before responding and then said in a low voice, "I think I might have got off on the wrong foot with Derek."

"What seems to be the problem?"

"The long and short of it is, I'm black, and he don' like black folk much, but there ain' no way dat boy's gonna run me off."

Olympia gulped a second time. It sounded strange hearing Norris, who was usually so articulate and well spoken, switch into, then right back out of, black dialect. She recalled her conversation with Paula just hours ago and suspected he was probably right. This was far more serious than she'd first suspected. Now what? She spoke with caution.

"Are you certain of this, Norris?"

Norris nodded. "Oh, yeah. Being black doesn't go away, Ma'am. You just get used to dealing with it. Some days are better than others. Everybody else up here is fine. It's just him."

"Is there some way I can be of help in this?" whispered Olympia.

"If and when I know, I'll tell you, but right now I'm just watching my back. He's a weird one, and I don't trust him. Some people are just plain mean, Chaplain, and I do believe he's one of them."

"Do you think one of us should speak to Brad?"

"Not yet, Ma'am." Norris looked both thoughtful and angry. "When the time is right, I surely will, but not yet."

Eighteen

On Wednesday afternoon Olympia left Orchards Cove and headed north once again toward Portland, wishing she were more excited about seeing John Stainer than she was. After all, he was intelligent and easy to talk to, and he did want to see her a second time. That had to count for something, at the very least a second chance. Then there was the Thai food. It would not be a wasted afternoon. Keep an open mind, she told herself.

While Olympia was rumbling along toward her lunch date, Paula Budreau was driving in the opposite direction on I-95, listening to the car radio and wondering what her visit with Spider was going to be like. He'd certainly sounded normal, whatever that was, when they talked on the phone. The more she thought about it, she realized she really didn't know him all that well, but what little she did know, she liked. Spider was a nice guy, but it seemed Derek had never missed a chance to belittle him or put him down.

Derek was as slippery as an eel. Any one action, in and of itself, seemed harmless enough. If someone did take issue or challenge him, he'd laugh it off, saying it was a joke or he was just kidding. Sometimes he'd even make further fun of his latest target by ridiculing them for having thin skin or suggesting they get a life. Still, was any of that enough to make someone make an attempt on his own life? That was the puzzling piece. Had something awful happened to Spider that no one was talking about? Had Derek or someone else at the Cove done something so mean spirited—no, make that downright evil—which pushed Spider over the edge? By now she thoroughly despised Derek, but all she could do about it was what Olympia had suggested: be watchful and take good notes.

Olympia found a public parking lot less than a block away from the address she'd written down, but when she rounded the corner onto Baker Street, she could see John Stainer standing in the doorway of what appeared to be a deserted restaurant. When she got closer, the big red sign that said Closed told her all she needed to know.

Bummer, she thought. She might not have been excited about her second meeting with John, but she was very much looking forward to the Thai food. Now what? Think positive. She smiled and waved to the sheepish looking man who awaited her.

"Hey, John, looks like our plans have been changed for us. What do you suggest? I know nothing about Portland, so you are not only my lunch date, you have just been appointed my tour guide."

"Geez, I'm sorry. I should have checked. What would you like to do?"

What I'd like is for you to make some suggestions, she thought with a mental scowl. "Anything you know of that's nearby? I'm easy."

He frowned. "Not offhand, but let me think." He brightened. "OK, I have an idea. Let's just walk around until we find something that appeals to us."

Oh, that's really original, she thought.

"Great idea," she said with an encouraging, toothy smile.

He looked puzzled. "Uh, you don't have a map, do you? I don't come down here very often. Portland is the big city as far as we Central Mainers go. In the summertime we tend to stay away from the crowds and the bustle."

Olympia did not roll her eyes. What she did do was take charge.

"OK, let's start by finding a map. They have to be everywhere. Big tourist business here, yes? After we get the map I suggest we find ourselves a sandwich shop, get a couple of sandwiches, walk down to the waterfront and eat them. We can sit and watch the boats and chat for a while, and then we can decide what to do next." Like how soon can I cut loose and get out of here, she thought. "How does that sound?"

"Perfect," said John. "Which way shall we walk?"

Olympia wet the tip of her finger and held it up in the breeze. "Logic says downhill goes toward the water and uphill goes away from the water. If we want to get to the harbor, we should probably walk downhill. Logic also says we'll probably find a deli or something along the way."

"You're amazing," said John.

"I certainly am," she muttered. "Come on then. The world is our oyster."

"I thought you wanted a sandwich?"

"I'm vegetarian," she answered.

The closer Paula got to the New Hampshire border, the more uncomfortable she was becoming, so much so that she pulled into a rest area to decide whether to keep on driving to Portsmouth or call and cancel and go back to Orchards Cove. The last thing she wanted to do was to hurt or disappoint Spider, but if she were to be completely honest with herself, she was feeling nervous about how she should act with him after all that had happened. Still, she reasoned with herself, his parents will be there, and if I'm really uncomfortable, I'll just leave. She checked the time. This little detour meant she was now running late. She'd better find a phone and give him a call.

Meanwhile, at his home in Portsmouth, Spider MacCormack was watching the clock. He was feeling healthier and stronger and surer of himself with every passing day. Walking the dog, working out and eating well were having the desired effect. He might not be gaining weight, but he was far more muscular and had much greater stamina. It was all part of his twofold plan to get back on his own two feet and go back to Orchards Cove and knock Derek Jamison completely off his. When he thought about it, his reasons for wanting to see Paula, besides liking her as a person and being grateful for her friendship, were also twofold. He wanted to see her for herself and spend time with her, but his sub-agenda, the one he wouldn't mention to her, was that she would be a conduit of information about Derek and his comings and goings at Orchards Cove.

He checked his watch for the umpteenth time. It was almost five; she should be here soon. Spider had decided to go out and wait on the front porch when he heard the telephone ring. With a sinking heart he picked up the receiver.

"Hello?"

"Spider? It's me, Paula. I'm running a little late, and I didn't want you to worry, OK? I had to stop for gas, and then I wanted a coffee, and it took longer than I thought. I should be there in about twenty minutes."

"Thanks for letting me know. I'll be outside on the front porch. The house is green with white shutters and white trim. It's the only green one on the street."

It was only after he hung up that Spider noticed just how fast his heart was thumping. He was really looking forward to seeing her, and it didn't seem long before she pulled up and parked next to the curb.

He double-jumped down the front steps and all but skipped over to open her door. All the while he was debating to hug her or not to hug her. He stopped himself. What the hell was he thinking? She was probably just feeling sorry for him, that's why she came.

Paula silenced the internal drama by initiating a giant hug and telling him how great he looked, then asking if she could please use the bathroom.

"I thought you stopped for gas and a coffee. I would have thought you'd have, uh ..."

"Well, I didn't, so show me where it is, and then we can talk."

Shortly thereafter, her bodily needs attended to, she and Spider were sitting side by side on the front porch on a squeaky double swing and drinking the iced tea Spider's mother had made for them. Paula was happily chattering on, telling him all the news and gossip from the Cove.

"They hired a guy named Norris to fill your place. He's an awesome guitar player. He helps out with the singing after supper and on Sunday morning sometimes. Derek is still a jerk. Since you left, he started picking on me and Norris when he gets the chance."

"What do you mean?" Spider stretched his arms out in front of himself and cracked his knuckles. He was the picture of casual relaxation.

"Well, between you and me, I think he's jealous of Norris, you know, the music thing. The other kids like him, too."

"How does he pick on you?"

She thought for a moment. "Hard to say. I think it's more an attitude thing. He mostly does it with dirty looks and crappy jobs. He ignores me if I make suggestions. And somehow he got the idea he could tell me who I could or could not be seen with and even told me I shouldn't be talking with Norris."

Bubbly Paula couldn't see Spider's clenched fists because he was sitting on them.

"Same old Derek." Then, changing the subject, "You hungry? I told my parents we might want to go into town for a pizza or something. What do you think?"

She flashed him a big smile. "Sure. I didn't think I was hungry until you mentioned food. Now all of a sudden, I'm starving. How far is it? I can drive, if you want."

"Nah, it's a nice walk. Have you ever walked around the old part of Portsmouth?"

"I've never walked around the new part of Portsmouth."

"You like historical stuff?" he asked.

"Well, it wasn't my favorite subject in high school, but I loved visiting Sturbridge Village and Plymouth Plantation. Is it anything like that, people in costumes and stuff?"

He nodded. "Kind of. The actors have probably gone home now, and most of the houses will be closed, but we can walk around and see it all. It's nice."

"And get a pizza?"

Spider looked over and grinned at her. "Yes, and get a pizza for the hungry girl. C'mon, just let me tell my folks we're going out and see if they want us to bring them back a take-out."

They did not, and Paula and Spider set off side by side at a comfortable pace.

The pizza place turned out to be a small, sit-down restaurant that did a heavy take-out trade, especially in the summer. The dining section was standard Italian restaurant décor: red and white checked table cloths, Chianti bottles with drippy candles and a garish, badly painted mural of what were likely intended to be Italian vineyards splashed across the back wall. The combined scents of tomato, basil and garlic, however, were the real thing and virtually intoxicating to a healthy young woman.

Once they were seated Spider announced this was his treat, and did Paula want a glass of wine or beer? She shook her head. "I'm not much of a drinker, and I won't even have one if I'm driving, but you go ahead, if you want to.

"I don't dare because of the meds I'm taking." It looked as though he was about to say something else but was interrupted by the table server bringing them their menus and asking for drink orders. Both ordered large Diet Cokes. When she returned a second time they ordered a large mushroom double cheese pizza with a side of anchovies for Paula. The server thanked them and said it would be about ten minutes.

Spider cleared his throat and took a sip of his Coke.

"Uh, Paula?"

"Mmmm?"

"About what happened ... that night at the Cove ..."

Paula wasn't sure she wanted to listen to this. At the same time, this poor guy had been through hell and back. The very least she could do was to hear him out. She looked up at her friend.

"Are you sure you want to talk about it, Spider?"

"I need to talk to somebody, Paula, and there's no one else I trust. Something happened that day that made me so mad I felt like I wanted to kill someone—Derek, of course. Then I realized that if I killed him, it wouldn't get me anything but life in prison, and that would have been worse than death, so I did what I thought was the only thing I could do, only I didn't make it. At first I was furious that I'd screwed it up, but now I'm really glad Brad came in and found me."

Paula reached across the table and took his hand in hers. She didn't know where this was going, but she was literally hanging onto him for dear life. "What happened?"

Spider flushed and struggled getting the words to come out.

"That morning, I thought I was alone in my room. I was looking at a porno magazine when Derek shoved open the door and caught me. I totally freaked and started crying, and of course, Derek started making fun of me for that, too."

Paula shuddered but said nothing to interrupt. As hard as it was to listen to this, she knew it was even harder for Spider to say it.

"I was beyond humiliated. I wanted to die right there and then, but it got worse. After he finished saying every kind of disgusting thing about me he could think of, he told me he was going to make sure everyone knew what I did in my spare time."

"Oh, for God's sake, guys are always looking at girlie magazines. My brother stuffs his under the mattress and thinks we don't know. We just look the other way. What's Derek's problem?"

"This wasn't a girlie magazine. It was guy magazine—a gay guy magazine. I'm gay, Paula, and you and Derek and the doctors at the hospital are the only people who know. My life has been a total hell. Ever since I was a little kid I knew I was different and wondered what I'd done wrong to get that way. By then the other kids were onto it, and it was constant name calling and sucker punches. Derek pushed me over the line that night, and it was a long time before I could be grateful that I lived. I got some good docs at the nut house—sorry, I shouldn't say that, at the hospital. I went to therapy every day and finally learned I didn't have to be cured. I am what I am, and what I am is normal for me. That was the first step. Once I got out, getting in touch with you was the second step, and now sitting here and saying all this is the third."

Paula took a sip of her Coke. She so wanted to do and say the right thing. It all made sense now, but there was so much more she didn't and perhaps never would understand. Why would anyone …?

"What's the next step?"

"No clue. I'm still in therapy. I need to come out to my parents, and I need to get my life on track. I'm planning to go back to school in the fall, and between now and then, I have six weeks or so to think about it. Needless to say there's some other stuff I need to deal with, but I'm not ready to talk about it. I'm still putting the pieces back together."

"I'm glad you told me, Spider."

"I'm glad, too. Everybody needs a friend they can trust, Paula. I haven't known you for very long, but from the beginning I just felt I could. I guess I was right. I'm skinny and geeky, and you treated me like a human being. I think Derek might have even been jealous. If he only knew." A flicker of a real smile lifted the corners of his lips just as their pizza arrived at the table.

Nineteen

When Paula got back to Orchard's Cove after her visit with Spider, it was well after ten. She tiptoed down the pine needle path to Olympia's site on the off chance she might still be up, but all was dark, so she turned around. There was no rush. She had a letter for Olympia that Spider asked her to deliver in person. He had given Paula permission to tell her about their conversation, and the letter was to thank her for staying with him that night. As much as she wanted to talk with Olympia, Paula was dead tired and glad to be heading for bed.

She knew the next day would be a busy one. The second to last full day of any successful conference was always a curious dichotomy of the campers wanting the experience to go on forever and already thinking about packing up. It made for lots of work and short tempers. Spider told her there was no rush about delivering the letter. More important was finding the time to stay with Olympia while she read it.

As it turned out Paula wasn't able to deliver the letter until late Saturday afternoon when the teens and their shaky sweat lodge were history, and the dance and music campers were mostly in and setting up. Earlier in the day Olympia had packed a bottle of good wine and some expensive English cheddar and Wensleydale in her cooler. Now she was happily awaiting Jim's imminent arrival when she heard footsteps on the path. She stood ready to greet her friend, but it was Paula.

"Got a minute?"

"Just a few. I'm expecting company, but I'm good till then. What's up? And by the way, how's Derek been acting lately?"

Paula shrugged and made a face. "Same old, same old. I just try and stay out of his way, and with all those kids running around this week, it was easy. Where do they get their energy?"

Olympia chuckled. "You're not that much older than they are, Paula, but now that I think of it, there are huge emotional and physical differences between fifteen to seventeen year olds and people in their early twenties."

"I'm twenty-two, actually, and yes, there is a difference. At least I hope I've calmed down. Anyway, Spider asked me to give you this and wanted me to stay with you while you read it."

What in the world, thought Olympia, holding out her hand to receive the letter.

Dear Chaplain Olympia,

This is to say thank you again for coming with me in the ambulance that night and staying with me in the hospital until my parents arrived. I know I was acting like a jerk and you were so kind anyway.

Everything was so jumbled up in my head I didn't know what I was thinking or saying. So if I said anything bad, I'm sorry. Anyway, Paula will tell you the rest of the story. I asked her to. And once again, thank you. You are a good person.

Love, Spider

Olympia refolded the letter and looked up at Paula. "How's he doing?"

Over the next several minutes, she told Olympia the good and the bad, word for heartbreaking word.

"That's vile," was Olympia's initial response when she heard what Derek had done. This was immediately followed by, "We need to talk with Brad."

Paula shook her head. "Spider asked me to tell you, but he made it clear he's not ready to do anything else right now. He hasn't told anyone but me."

Olympia understood. "But we do need to find a way to deal with Derek. We can't have him getting away with this kind of behavior."

"He's sneaky. He does just enough to make you miserable but not enough to get caught or get himself fired."

Unless Spider came forward, there was nothing Paula or anyone else could do. Olympia shook her head in frustration. Damn, she thought.

"Just keep your eyes and ears open, Paula, and keep taking notes." She didn't say anything about the conversation she'd had with Norris earlier in the week, but maybe it was time to have another one. One way or another she was going expose that bully Derek for what he was.

This sort of thing was not in her job description, but it was in her life description. Olympia was congenitally unable to remain still or silent in the face of injustice or wrongdoing. It was why she had become a minister and why she remained on at Merriwether College. It was her way of making a difference in the world around her. It was her way of making things right. It was what made her get up in the morning and just as often what kept her awake long into the night.

"Is that a familiar voice I hear?" said a pleasant and resonant man's voice.

Olympia leaped out of her chair, knocking it over in the process, and squashed her friend Jim in a giant bear-hug. Father Jim, Roman Catholic priest, was out of uniform and wearing freshly ironed chino pants, a blue plaid shirt and brown leather loafers without socks. He looked gorgeous.

"Jim, this is Paula Budreau, she works here. Paula, this is my best friend ever, Jim Sawicki."

Paula smiled, shook his hand and made her excuses. It was clear the two friends had some catching up to do.

"Let's check in after the weekend, OK, Paula?"

"You say when, I'm not going anywhere. Nice to meet you, Jim. I'll be off now. It's crew supper time, and I'm starving."

Olympia had been so excited at the prospect of Jim joining her for a week that she had actually been counting down the hours until he arrived. Now that he was standing there in front of her, she was at a loss for words. Where should she begin? Relax, she reminded herself. There's time.

"Cold water or chilled wine, monsieur?"

"*Tous les deux s'il'vous plait.*" Then he switched to English. Both, please, and in that sequence. It was a long, dry ride through the center of Boston when I and everyone else in Massachusetts decided to get out of town and head north. I've been on the road for three and a half hours."

"Ugh." Olympia winced in sympathy and went off to get their drinks. First she filled an empty peanut butter jar with water, and while Jim was making short work of it, she filled two jelly jars with a better than average Sauvignon Blanc. Jim held his jar up to the light and eyed the contents.

"Mmm, nice pattern. Waterford, I believe? Must be a new one, though, I'm not familiar with it."

"Shut up and drink it before I pour ZaRex in it. For your information, I do happen to have some Waterford back home, but I'm not fool enough to bring it up here."

Jim sniffed the contents of his jelly jar and wrinkled his nose. "One should use only the best crystal when serving a good wine. One enhances the other. Hey, not bad!"

Olympia managed to laugh and groan at the same time, and then she held up her own jar.

"It's good stuff, I promise. Cheers, Jim. I've missed you."

The two settled into Olympia's new camp chairs with wine in hand and a plate with the cheeses and a party assortment of crackers carefully balanced on a tree stump between them. Olympia explained that other than the hour she had to spend at the weekly orientation meeting with the new conferees, the night was theirs. If he wished they could eat in the dining hall, or if he preferred, once she'd discharged her staff duties, they could go out to one of the nearby restaurants. For a resort and vacation area, she explained with a knowing smile, a number of the local restaurants were really very good. Jim surprised her when he said he'd just as soon eat in tonight.

"I've seen all I want to of the inside of a car, my dear. I want fresh air and sunshine and then maybe a barefoot walk on the beach. I can't begin to tell you how good it feels to be out of the city. It'll take me a day or two to shake it all off. After that we'll go out to one of those restaurants you mentioned or maybe even do a comparison study of several of them. Culinary research, of course."

Jim held up his jelly jar a second time and took a large and appreciative swallow. "Mmmm, not bad, Olympia. Not bad at all for a Protestant."

Olympia fired a wadded-up napkin in his general direction.

Dinner, considering it was nonprofit camp food, was really delicious. The cook did one hell of a lasagna, one with meat and one all vegetable, and Jim, Mr. Moderation himself, even had seconds. The earth-mother in Olympia, the part of her that fussed over all living things, was pleased and hoped to fatten him up a bit over the week.

She introduced him around the table as Jim, no last name, an old friend who would be staying the week in the hotel. She noticed, as did Jim, that a few appraising eyebrows lifted, and a few sly winks could be observed, but Olympia and Jim just smiled and nodded. Let them think what they want. Gossip was the national pastime up here, so why not give them something different to chew on? Olympia looked away and stifled a giggle. She could see they were itching to know more, but the imp in her said, let them wonder. We all need a little mystery in our lives, do we not?

Twenty

Later that evening, after the dining hall singing and community vespers, Olympia and Jim left their shoes at the end of the boardwalk and set off for a twilight walk along the beach. The faint sounds of the first evening of music and dance drifted over and around them, growing fainter as they walked along the water's edge. It doesn't get much better than this, thought Olympia. She tucked her arm through Jim's, and the two walked along in silence for several minutes. Eventually Jim disengaged his arm and reached down to pick up a sand dollar. Even in the fading light the bleached white of the surface made it easy to spot. He carefully brushed off the sand and pocketed it.

"Something to remind me of this place and time, and now tell me what's happening with you. I know you came up here to do some thinking. Have you made any life-altering decisions?"

The truth was, she had, but which of those to share, even with Jim? Start with the most innocuous and take it from there.

"So I've had two dates with a man I met through a personal ad."

He stopped short. "You what?"

She grinned. "Yup, but nothing exciting to report. No sparks. We may or may not have another date, but even now, the more I think of it, probably not. He's OK, but it's not worth pursuing. I did get another response, though. This one is a college professor, or at least he says he is. Likes travel, reading and quiet walks on the beach. Why do they all say they like quiet walks on the beach? Why can't men just be honest and say they are looking for someone who is discreet, independently wealthy and twenty-five years younger than they themselves admit to being? Nope, quiet reading and walks on the beach."

Jim laughed. "Probably because they can't think of anything else to say, and it sounds reasonably romantic while at the same time nonthreatening. It's a standard opening gambit in my world, too, or at least it was before I entered the priesthood."

Olympia blinked in the darkness. Jim rarely made reference to his life before the priesthood. She knew he'd had one, and she knew that on the few times he did reference it, it made him terribly sad.

"So no excitement on the social or romantic front," he continued. "Then how about this? How is Orchards Cove treating you?"

She chuckled. "How much do you want to know, and how long have you got?"

"Everything and as long as you want. I'm here for a week, remember. You don't have to get it all into one walk on the beach."

She considered where to start. "This was supposed to be a summer of reflection, but it seems a lot more like duck and cover. Although I must say, things seemed to have calmed down considerably since the first two weeks."

"Details, Olympia, I need details, chapter and verse. Start at the beginning."

And so she began with Spider's unsuccessful leap off his dresser, her ride with him to the hospital and, according to a mutual friend, how he seemed to be getting better. After that she gave him a blow-by-blow description of the thunderstorm from hell, her table-top entrapment and eventual chain saw rescue. The crew and staff now referred to it as their personal campground Armageddon. Have I missed anything, she thought? Yes, maybe more about John Stainer. On second thought, maybe not.

It was full dark now, and Olympia suggested they turn and head back. While it was not possible to get totally lost, since the beach only went north and south, it was very possible to miss the end of the boardwalk in the dark. She'd done it before.

As they padded along, skirting the wavelets and splashing in others, she told him about Derek, the bully crew boss, and how difficult it was to deal with him. On the one hand, she pointed out, he was really good at getting tasks done around the campus, but too often at the cost of crew morale. Both she and Brad, the camp director, were struggling with that one. If Jim had any suggestions, she'd welcome them.

"Bullies are everywhere, Olympia. You wouldn't think a priest or a monk or a nun would be a bully, but I think sometimes they are the worst, and they usually get away with it because people are intimidated and afraid to report it. I went to Catholic schools all my life, and believe me, there were nuns and priests out there who should never have been allowed near a little kid."

"You're not telling me anything. I grew up in a mostly Catholic neighborhood, and the kids were all terrified of the nuns. On the other hand, I had some pretty rotten lay teachers and camp counselors. Power just seems to affect some people very badly. Why is it, Jim?"

"If there was a definitive cause and answer to that, I'd be a rich man. I do know that a common trait of bullies is underlying fear of inadequacy and explosive anger if anyone gets close to figuring it out. The other common factor is a history of childhood abuse and domestic violence and the total helplessness that goes along with that kind of experience. Many bullies feel so terribly inadequate that they beat up on anything smaller or weaker than themselves in order to have some sense of power and control. It's sad and twisted, but it's human. I wish there were an answer or a cure. When I was in social work, we were just beginning to try and come up with programs to deal with it, but we knew we were looking at the tip of the iceberg. To say it's complicated is a gross understatement."

"Is that because people like that don't often get caught or called out?"

"That's certainly one aspect of it. People don't rat on each other. You know what kids do to squealers. Peer pressure and the need to fit in are very effective in controlling a group of people." Jim discreetly covered a yawn. "Let's talk more about this tomorrow when I'm more awake."

"Oh, look, I think I see the boardwalk. I wonder what time it is."

Jim pushed a button on his watch, and his wrist began to glow. "It's eleven o'clock."

As if on cue, Olympia covered a huge yawn of her own.

"I'll walk you back to your site, Olympia."

"Oh, that's OK, Jim. The paths are lighted, and the only thing I need to watch out for is a skunk or a raccoon, and they know me. I do it all the time."

"Any snakes up here?"

"I'm surprised you ask. Not many, all harmless, and they pretty much keep to themselves."

"Good," said Jim. "I don't like snakes."

Olympia patted Jim on the arm. "You're safe with me."

"Oh, good, I feel much better now."

This time she smacked him and chuckled. "Goodnight, Jim. I'm really glad you're here."

"Me, too."

With that, Olympia gave her friend a quick hug and started down the hill, thinking about snakes and wondering how the poor things got such a bad name. Oh, yes, she thought, I think I remember reading something about it in Genesis.

The next morning Olympia and Jim sat together at breakfast, but after that, she told him he was on his own until four in the afternoon.

"Not a problem. It's a beautiful day, and what I'd really like to do is go check out some of the galleries and antique shops I saw along Route 1."

"Oh, there are plenty of those, all right, but most of them are tourist traps. However, there is some wheat amongst the chaff. I know you know what you're looking at, so have at it. I'll see you at happy hour."

"What did you say the name of Mr. Bully is?"

"Why, what do you have in mind?"

"I can look at just so many antique shops. you know. I might come back here after lunch so I can wander around and maybe check him out. So what's his name?"

Olympia dropped her voice. "Derek Jamison, but won't that be a little obvious? You can't very well stalk him, you know."

Jim waved off her concerns. "I'm a guest of the establishment, I'm out exploring the campus, and I shall be the very picture of innocence. Trust me."

"If anyone can do it, I guess you can, Father."

Jim winked and lifted his index finger to his lips. "Shhhh."

The rest of Olympia's day was pleasantly busy. In the morning she had a meeting with the music and dance people to plan a couple of the vespers services, and in the afternoon, Brad had asked her to meet with him privately to discuss Derek's behavior. She reluctantly agreed, knowing there was much she couldn't say because she was bound by confidentiality.

They both knew Derek was a problem, and any dialogue on the subject was better than none. Hadn't Brad actually mentioned it before she'd even come up there? They both had hoped this would be a summer of growth for him, but at the halfway point it wasn't looking good. She knew well the object of any exercise in human relations is to start by acknowledging a person's strengths so they will be open to hearing constructive suggestions. The difficulty was always getting the message across without setting the person off.

In this case Derek was likely to go on the defensive because someone on the crew had been complaining. On the other hand, maybe it was time to lower the boom and set the boy straight, which, without solidly documented evidence involving the aggrieved, would not be possible. Olympia was not feeling too positive when she tapped at Brad's office door.

Twenty-One

At four that afternoon Jim was walking down the path to Olympia's site with a bottle of something expensive under his arm. The cats, which had now been given free-run privileges when she was at the site, ran out, tails held high, to greet him. Olympia got out the jelly jars.

"Oh, no you don't," said Jim, setting his parcel on the tree stump. "Despite all efforts to the contrary, I'm going to improve the ambiance around here. He unwrapped the package and produced one bottle of a very good Pinot Noir and two real wine glasses with stems and everything.

Olympia giggled. "You'll make a lady of me yet, Jim."

"I'm not going that far. Say, do you have any of those cheeses and crackers left? This calls for a little comestible enhancement."

Olympia came back from the food chest with a puzzled look on her face. "I thought I did, but I guess we must have finished everything yesterday."

"You didn't forget and leave it out, did you?"

She shook her head. "No, I've been living in the woods too long to do that. I double secure everything, but now that I think about it, I was pretty excited to have you here. I suppose I could have forgotten and made a raccoon or a skunk really happy with all that free food. It's not the end of the world."

Jim made a dismissive gesture with his free hand. "Never mind, we'll pick something up when we go out. This wine can stand on its own."

When the two had settled down with full glasses, Jim related his adventures as a tourist in civilian clothes. He had indeed noodled through several antique/junk stores and managed to find one amid the dross that really was worth stopping for. It was there that he'd bought the wine glasses. He went south as far as Ogunquit, and not unlike the selection of antique stores along the way, the art and fine craft galleries ranged in content and quality from downright lovely all the way to places sporting red velvet lobsters and plastic clamshell sunglasses. But it been a good day, and Jim was content and tired. He'd gotten back far later than he'd originally planned and thus had no time to do any casual observation of crew and staff.

"No probs," said Olympia. "That was a side bar anyway. You're on vacation, Jim, make the most of it." She raised her glass in his direction.

"So how did your day go?" said Jim.

"Well, I had that meeting with Brad, and there is a little trouble brewing in River City."

Jim looked mystified.

"It's a reference to *The Music Man*. The people in the music and dance conference are putting together a concert version of it as part of the main activity of the week. They'll do it this Saturday, and you'll still be here, so you can see it with me. It should be great. Do you know the show?"

"Not really. I'm not a huge fan of musical theater. But back to Mr. Bully. What did this Brad person have to say?"

She made a face. "Basically we're in that never-never land of knowing it's going on but not quite able to do anything about it. We need someone to actually come forward and complain, say something specific. I've heard grumblings, and so has Brad, but nothing we can pinpoint. You know how tight kids can be. They might really dislike someone, but they still won't speak up."

"Only too well, Olympia. The whole damn Catholic Church has elevated keeping ugly secrets to a fine art. It makes me sick, but being who and what I am, I'm totally unable to say anything."

The conversation had taken a very dark turn.

"Is that because you're gay, Jim?"

"Me and plenty of others like me, and we're all holding each other hostage."

"If it's that bad, why do you stay? I know plenty of priests who have left. It's not a disgrace anymore."

"I'm not ready to go that far, at least not yet. Somewhere deep inside, the idealist in me is still alive. This is what I've wanted to be since I was in grade school. It is the way I believe I can make some sort of meaning of my life. There are many wonderful priests in the Catholic Church, Olympia. I still want to be one of them." He paused for a sip of wine. "I took a detour when I met Paul, but I picked it up again after he died. I'm a priest now. I've taken holy orders, and I intend to honor them."

Then, by way of changing the subject, Jim held up his glass and swirled the remaining wine in the afternoon light. "Beautiful legs on this one."

"If you say so," said Olympia. "Should I take that as a compliment?"

"Much good it does me," said Jim with a wistful smile. "Sorry about that, I got way too heavy. Let's think about where we're going to have dinner."

Olympia smiled gently at her friend. He'd opened his personal door another inch wider and allowed her to peek further inside.

In Portsmouth, New Hampshire, Spider was right on schedule—his own personal schedule. With each passing day he looked and felt stronger and was taking more and more control of his days and nights. This evening he was going to have The Talk with his parents. He suspected they might already know, but it had never been mentioned. On the other hand, hadn't his mother been crazy happy when she heard Paula was coming to visit? Maybe she didn't know. What will be, will be, he told himself. Since it was his parents' custom to have a single glass of wine after supper, he'd wait until then to ask if he might join them for a little while.

The Green Being was everything Jim promised, a delightful and funky vegan restaurant with as many menu choices as Olympia had ever encountered in her twenty years of being a strict vegetarian. She was, in fact, an ovo-lacto, vegetarian, meaning she did eat eggs and dairy, but she didn't even whisper these two words within earshot of any of the staff there. She was in vegetable heaven as she happily examined the newspaper sized menu. Vegan meant no animal products whatsoever. She could live with that. Besides, they had a wine list that even Jim was impressed with. This would be a night to remember. Olympia had gone so far as to dress for the occasion. She wore the same outfit that she had worn for her lunch with John Stainer, light slacks and the same loose gauzy top that would allow her to enjoy a full meal without further adjustments. Jim had on a light blue short-sleeved shirt and white slacks. She smiled. He was one good lookin' dude.

Spoiled for choice, Olympia eventually settled on roasted vegetables baked in a puff pastry with an arugula based salad, with pureed cantaloupe and fresh mint soup as an appetizer.

Jim ordered two stuffed Portobello mushrooms, a multi-grain salad, and carrot and ginger soup. It was only then that they could order their wine, a bright crisp Soave recommended by the sommelier, which, he promised, would perfectly complement their choices. Olympia was over the top. Good food, great wine, her best friend and a whole evening ahead of them. It was only when the sommelier returned and almost imperceptibly brushed his hand against Jim's shoulder before he left that she crash-landed back into the immediate present. She hadn't missed what just happened, and she was lost for words.

"Did he …?"

Jim treated it with a dismissive wave. "It happens, Olympia. I just won't pick up on it. He'll get the message. If I was going to respond, I'd make some sort of signal, and he'd come back and slip me his phone number."

"Doesn't that … I mean, you're sitting with me, for God's sake. Maybe you should have worn your priest suit? I don't believe it." She was still floundering.

"Relax, Olympia. He's buying, I'm not selling. It's over. Let's try that wine."

Two hours later the two had worked their way to the bottom of the bottle and were now judiciously having coffee and dessert before getting back into Jim's car. They both ordered lemon sorbet on wedges of lemon sponge cake with claret sauce, and black coffee. Olympia held up her fork.

"I can't thank you enough for this evening, Jim. I didn't know how much I needed it until now. Orchards Cove is lovely, but it's pretty intense sometimes."

"Any small, tight group gets that way. You should see the nitpicking and bickering that goes on at the college, priests and professors scrapping over bones." He shook his head. "You'd think they'd know better."

"I can relate to that. I suppose that's one of the reasons I'm thinking about getting out of academia altogether." She paused. "But I suppose that kind of crap goes on everywhere."

Jim nodded. "It does. You just have to make a decision to step over or around it and not let any of it stick to your shoe. Being gay or straight has nothing to do with it. It's just people being people, and it's sad."

Olympia laid her hand over Jim's. "You don't have to answer this, but who is, or was, Paul? You mentioned him earlier today when we were back at the campsite."

Jim paused. "Where to begin? He's the man I fell in love with and left seminary for. He was the love of my life."

"What happened?"

Jim shook his head, and his eyes filled with tears. "He died of AIDS at the height of the epidemic in the eighties. I wanted to go with him, but it wasn't my time. Eventually I pulled myself together and went back to seminary. When I completed my studies, I took my vows of poverty, obedience and chastity, and for the foreseeable future I plan on honoring them."

"Oh, Jim," was all she could say in response.

"We've all got broken places, Olympia. Now you know where mine is."

Later that evening, sitting side by side on the breakwater and listening to the sound of the waves, Olympia told Jim about the daughter she gave up for adoption when she was seventeen.

Twenty-Two

By midsummer Olympia understood how the conferences followed a semi-predictable ebb-and-flow pattern. There was a flurry of activity at the beginning followed by a settling in. If there was going to be a problem other than weather, it usually happened on Wednesday. This could be a misunderstanding, staffing issues, sometimes disputes over the food, or in one memorable case, recycling practices. According to Brad, who was familiar with recent history, some groups were more prone to conflict than others, with ministers often being the worst.

When Olympia asked him why, he said, "They want to do everything themselves, and then when something doesn't work, they blame us. Maybe because they put so many demands on themselves, they have less tolerance for imperfections in others." He shrugged his shoulders. "We get through it. This one, Music and Dance, is always a breeze. Everybody has fun with these guys, they're great." He was right on the mark. It was a wonderful week and perfect for Jim to enjoy. She was so glad he'd accepted her invitation. Jim could take life and himself too seriously sometimes. Over the last few days, she'd never seen him so unbuttoned, and she loved it.

The remainder of the music and dance conference was, as predicted, easy and enjoyable. Everyone on campus was looking forward to the performance at the end of the week, and by Thursday the familiar words and routines from the musical score could be heard everywhere and at all hours.

Even Jim, despite his professed disinterest in musical theater, told Olympia he was looking forward to seeing it.

By Saturday the place was a beehive of activity and antics. Norris had been enlisted to be part of the pit orchestra, which consisted of an upright piano, a set of borrowed drums, Norris on electric guitar, and two hopeful recorders. Scene painters, with the help of the crew, were doing their best to create a midwestern town. The costume crew had scoured every thrift shop and yard sale within twenty miles, resulting in flashes of bonnets, regimental stripes and dirndl skirts that could be seen flying in all directions. The excitement was palpable, and everyone was caught up in it. Almost everyone.

Derek was going through the motions, but he was clearly distracted by the dramatic confusion and the universal disregard of schedule and daily routine created by multiple rehearsals. Every day he did as he was asked and stayed on top of his crew. He'd seen it all before. At the end of the week, the place would go wild for one night, and the next day they'd all be under the gun to clean it up in time for the next conference to check in.

But ever since Brad had told him to lighten up, he'd been troubled. He felt as if he were being watched, that someone was out there waiting for him to screw up. Then there was the snake thing. He was getting more and more paranoid about that, seeing them everywhere. It was getting worse. Maybe he'd made a mistake in coming up here, but if he had, it was too late. Derek was not a failure, and he was not a quitter. He just needed a different approach. Maybe he was being too heavy handed, or maybe they were all a bunch of pansy-assed wimps, and to hell with them. Either way, he would make it through the summer, no matter what.

Spider was doing his best to make it through the summer, as well. Since coming out, life at home was easier. With his plans to go back to school in the fall in place and a daily routine of chores around the house, regular exercise and healthy eating, he was slowly regaining his parents' trust and confidence. So when he asked if he might take a couple of days off by himself toward the end of the summer and stay in his grandfather's hunting camp less than an hour north of there, they were doubtful and worried. But when he assured them this would be part of his healing process, time alone with himself and their faith in him to be able to handle it, he was finally able to convince them to let him go.

"There's no phone in the cottage, but I'll call you collect every night from a pay phone in town."

"I can't help but worry, but I'd feel better if you did that," said his mother. When she offered to pack him some groceries and maybe send along a pot of chili, he smiled and ruffled her hair as he declined.

"No, thanks, Mama-bear. I can't say why, but I just need to do this all by myself. I think it's kind of a rite of passage for me, even if it's only for a few days. I'll be OK, I promise. And if I'm not, I'll come home. I promise that, too." That did it. They agreed and wished him well.

Later, alone in his room, Spider took out his journal and reviewed his notes. It took exactly one hour and forty-five minutes to drive from his house to the state park just north of Orchards Cove. He knew this because he'd practiced it several times when his parents thought he was just out driving around. Timing was everything now, and Spider would need to make the most of every minute.

The next day, day Paula bounced into Olympia's campsite to report that she'd been to see Spider again. He seemed to be doing really well and asked to be remembered to Olympia, "and oh, by the way, he came out to his parents."

When she paused to take a breath, Olympia raised a curious eyebrow and asked. "How did that go?"

"Pretty good, I guess. He said they weren't surprised to hear it. His mom got a little teary but said she loved him anyway. Anyway what?" she sputtered. "I hate when people say that: I like you anyway. It means they don't really, but they're saying it because they think they have to, don't you agree?"

"You may have a point," said Olympia. She was thinking that Paula might be a rapid fire talker, but she was wiser than her years. "I'm glad he did it. It couldn't have been easy. Make sure you give him my regards the next time you see him."

"Oh, I will. He always asks for you. Come to think of it, he always asks about Derek, too."

"What was he asking?" Olympia inquired. She was doing her best to look noncommittal.

Paula waggled her shoulders as she thought about it. "Spider wanted to know if Derek was still bugging me, or if he'd said anything else to Norris about hanging out with me. I told him he seems to have backed off. But now that you've got me thinking about it, I have to say he's jumpy as anything—Derek, I mean. It's weird. If you come up behind him, and he doesn't hear you, he leaps out of his skin. I don't know what's going on. He probably needs a day off as much as anything. Does he get time off like the rest of us?"

"I think so, said Olympia. "At least he's supposed to, but maybe he doesn't take it. I'll check with Brad."

"Hey, I gotta go. You going to that play Saturday night? They actually got me to be in the chorus. Can you believe it? Costume, dance routine and everything."

"I wouldn't miss it. In fact, I'm bringing my friend Jim with me."

"Is he that cute guy that's been staying up in the hotel? The one who sits with you in the dining hall?"

"That's the one," said Olympia.

The rest of Jim's week at Orchards Cove was mostly spent reading on the porch, reading on the beach and walking in the woods in and around the campground with a book under his arm. When Olympia could get free, the two patronized some of the local restaurants, looked for odd treasures in the ubiquitous antique shops and second-hand book stores, and slowly told one another more of their stories.

It was on one of those jaunts that Olympia brought up the subject of Spider MacCormack. Jim had always been her go-to person when something was troubling her, and even though things at Orchards Cove seemed to be as good as they could be, she still couldn't get Spider completely out of her mind. She would never forget his pale face on the pillow, afraid to die and at the same time furious that he hadn't. Of course he'd put on a good face to Paula and his parents, but what was he thinking when he was alone?

On Saturday afternoon, the day before Jim would go back to Dorchester and put on his priest clothes again, and the rest of the Cove was awhirl with pre-performance high spirits, Olympia suggested they go on a beach walk. The tide was well out, so walking on the hard-packed sand was easy on the legs and offered no end of treasures to be picked up and examined.

"Have I mentioned Spider MacCormack to you?"

"I've heard you say the name. Isn't he the one who tried to commit suicide at the beginning of the summer?"

Olympia stopped, picked up a smooth flat stone, wound up and let it fly. It skipped a whole three times before disappearing. Jim was not about to let that go unchallenged. He looked around and carefully selected a similar stone. Then he rinsed it off, tossed it up and caught it and weighed it in each hand. Only then did he take aim at a distant point somewhere between the two of them and the horizon and fire it off. Seven skips, and Jim flashed a triumphant thumbs-up. Olympia rolled her eyes.

Without another word Jim brushed the wet sand off his hands and dried them on the back of his shorts. "So what about Spider MacCormack?"

She began with the unsuccessful suicide attempt, the observed bullying on the part of Derek, Spider's growing friendship with Paula, and his coming out first to her and then to his parents. She finished with his apparent steady recovery.

Jim bit his lip and shook his head. "Poor kid. I can relate to all of it. I never got so far as to want to take my own life over who and what I am, but I know more than one poor devil that has. In my family the priesthood was the perfect answer. Don't ask, don't tell, look the other way, and don't make trouble. In other words, don't embarrass us."

"Until you met Paul."

Jim nodded. "Then all hell broke loose. It was as if I'd died. Nobody in my family ever walked away from the priesthood, not back then anyway. I never said why other than I needed time to think. I kept Paul a secret from my straight friends, and if they suspected, they were kind enough not to say it. The worst was when I was in high school. Young people can be so cruel. The kids were unrelenting, and the pedophile priests were lurking in the shadows, watching and waiting. I had to watch every step I took."

"So why in God's name did you go back?"

"You just said it, in God's name. The church was the only truth I knew back then. I knew that as a gay man there was a place for me as long as I kept quiet. I did and I have and I will continue to do so. But we were talking about Spider, and I ran on about myself. Sorry about that."

"I'm glad you did, Jim. It's not exactly the same, but all those years ago, I had only one choice with my daughter, and that was to put her out of my life and never speak of it. It's haunted me every day of my life since."

"The silent searing pain of shame," said Jim.

Olympia could only nod. When she got her voice back she told Jim that was probably the reason why she kept worrying about Spider. She understood what it was like to have a secret you could never tell.

"But from what you say he seems to be coming along," said Jim.

"That's what he tells his friend Paula, who tells me what he wants us to hear."

"You must have made some impression for him to want to keep in touch with you."

"I don't know, Jim. Maybe somewhere in that haze of pain that night, he understood that I got it, because I did. Not that he was gay, but that something had happened to him that pushed him over the edge. I know it sounds almost corny, but it's the language of the heart. They don't teach it in seminary, but if we are going to be any good at this priesthood/ministry thing we have to be able to understand it, don't we?"

Jim just nodded.

"We keep getting off the subject. Should I just step away from Spider and let him come see me if he wants to?"

"Right in one. I can see why you feel such concern, but in the end, you're not family, you're not his straight best friend, and you only met because were thrown together in tragic circumstances. You need to move on, Olympia. If he wants or needs further contact, let him initiate it. There may well be a part of him that is grateful to you and at the same time never wants to see you again because you know too much."

There was nothing to say other than, "Thanks, Jim, I guess I needed that."

"Permission to do the same for me."

After supper Jim and Olympia joined everyone else on campus in the knotty pine paneled multipurpose room that tonight was made over into a theater. For stage productions it was fitted out with a dusty blue velvet curtain, a few make-do lights, and a portable twelve-inch-high platform which could be set down and locked into place to act as a stage.

At other times this malleable room was a dance hall, banquet hall or ballroom, depending on the event, and in case of rainy weather, a game room or indoor gym. The acoustics were unforgiving, the chairs old and squeaky, and the lack of air conditioning required a rank of ancient ceiling fans permanently turned on high to keep air in the place at least moving. But it was tradition, and the devoted regulars wouldn't change a thing.

Fortunately for the actors and the audience, the night was pleasant, and happy anticipation was running high on either side of the curtain. Jim and Olympia seated themselves near the back and waited as the room slowly filled with campers and crew and kitchen staff and administrative staff who were all magically transformed into an audience.

"Let the festivities begin," whispered Jim.

"Hang on, my friend, nothing ever starts on time up here except meals."

Then, with an uncertain flourish from the pick-up orchestra, the curtains were pulled open, and slowly the magic began to fill the room. Olympia was transported, and even Jim, who could be a bit of an arts snob, was soon caught up in the fun and tapping his foot along with the seventy-six trombones.

At the end he stood and cheered with everyone else, amazed and delighted by how a dedicated group of people in less than a week could pull all this together. If not exactly a theatrical triumph, it was certainly a theatrical amazement and well deserving of the standing ovation that exploded at the end of final number.

"That was terrific," said Jim. He was smiling broadly.

"I'll make sure I tell Paula and Norris how great you thought it was. I can't belicve it. They all worked so hard to pull it together, and they did it. They are going to be wiped out tomorrow."

"Now that you mention it, I think I have a horizontal date with St. Mattress myself," said Jim.

"It's all that clapping and cheering, Jim. It tires you out."

They parted company in front of the hotel, she to go to her tent in the woods and he to his single bed on the second floor. As she walked down the hill she smiled at the memory of Jim's display of happy and carefree enthusiasm. It was not something she got to see very often. She was so glad he'd come. He needed to get away from the strictures of the priestly life once in a while, didn't he?

Twenty-Three

The next morning, Sunday, was changeover day. The music and dance folks, happy and exhausted, were clearing up and moving out. Much to Derek's relief there was far less mess to clean up than he'd anticipated. The campers had done a very good job of it themselves, and so it was mostly the general chaos of the comings and goings and inevitable mini-crises of same which by midsummer they were used to. Derek was feeling better. He needed some sense of order, structure and routine, and as amorphous as a changeover day was, there was a certain predictability to it. By suppertime the worst was over.

In his room on the hill Jim was up and packed before breakfast and stayed on only long enough after that to attend the Sunday service. He and Olympia didn't often get to see the other in action, so to speak, because as clergy they both usually worked on Sundays. She'd gone with him to a Christmas midnight mass once, and he'd gone to an interfaith event where she was preaching, but for the most part their active clerical lives were separate. After the service they parted with hugs and promises to write and/or call. Then, much to Olympia's surprise, Jim told her that if he got the chance, he might come back for a mid-week getaway. He had no more Sundays off.

She waved him off and stood and watched until his old Toyota rounded the bend and disappeared.

"He seems nice. You're going to miss him." It was Paula.

"Oh, hi, Paula, and yes, I will miss him, but he had a great time. He said he might even come back before the end of the summer."

"Is he your boyfriend? Oops, I mean if you don't mind my asking. Geez, it's none of my business. I'm sorry."

Olympia chuckled. "Relax. Of course you can ask. He's not my boyfriend, just a very special best friend."

"Ohhh, I get it," said Paula.

I don't think you do, thought Olympia, but other than a sweet smile, she offered nothing more on the subject.

By early that afternoon the ministers were moving in and immediately taking charge of everything, starting with the outdoor chapel. They wanted to create their own worship space, so they set about draping it with scarves and banners and the symbols of every known religion they could find or create, and that was just the beginning. I hope we don't get any rain, thought Olympia as she watched them in full swing and swag and drape. Then she reminded herself that it was not her problem.

Despite the fact that it was a Sunday, Derek was definitely feeling less stressed. By now the crew knew their routine. He'd put himself in charge of the campground registration and settling in and had three crew guys to help with the tent-pitching and camper-leveling, if needed. This way he was in the office for all to see and hear but nowhere near where he might be surprised by a wayward snake. He made a specific point of thanking his crew whenever possible and smiling at new guests as they drove into the entrance. To all appearances, he was back on his game.

For the first time in a long time, Spider was feeling truly optimistic. Everything was going according to plan, his plan.

By this time next week he'd be heading out on his own driving north, no questions asked. His destination was a state park in south coastal Maine less than a mile north of Orchards Cove.

Jim's ride home was just as tedious as the ride up had been. As he crawled along he promised himself the next time he went up there, and there would be a next time, it would be in the middle of the week and the middle of the day. It had been a long time since Jim had stepped out of harness and left the black shirt and socks at home and found himself generally ignored by the people he encountered. It was different, but was it a difference he might want to get used to? Jim didn't have an answer for that.

As had been predicted, the week following Jim's visit was a very light one for Olympia work-wise. The place was awash with a blessing of ministers. Brad had offered to let her sign up and join the conference free of charge, if she wanted to, but that sounded too much like the postman's day off to Olympia. This was another one of her mother's sayings, and it referred to the mailman, who on his day off, and for a change of pace, always went for a nice long walk. Nope, if she was going to have an easy week, she might just vacate the place entirely for a night or two. Places like Orchards Cove, where intense people are living in close proximity, can become much too ingrown toward the end of the season, and by early August Olympia was definitely beginning to feel the pinch. A day or two away from there in a different setting would do her a power of good.

She briefly thought about calling John Stainer but crossed it off before she completed the thought. Pleasant as he was, that's all he was—better than playing solitaire or watching old movies but not by much. She realized there wasn't even a glimmer of a spark where he was concerned and then and there decided there was no point in seeing him again. So, Reverend Doctor, what shall we do, she asked herself? She was in the state of Maine, and surely some of the tourist brochures she'd picked up over the summer would offer something. Lo and behold, she found it, less than an hour away and affordable.

That very afternoon, with Brad's permission and blessing, she booked herself a bare-basics vacation cabin boasting of indoor plumbing and electricity on a scenic pond, no AC, bring your own table fan and linens. There was no mention of free mosquitoes, but just in case, she packed her most potent bug spray. If Norris and Paula agreed to look after the cats, Olympia would sign herself up for forty-eight hours of solitary freedom. There would be time to catch up with herself and give some time to thinking about the questions she'd brought up there along with her camping gear: her future in academia and/or the church, either, neither or both? Male companionship was on temporary hold. There was only one telephone at Pond Side Cabins, and she had no intention of going near it. Brad said she could take Tuesday and Wednesday nights away and plan to be back, refreshed and renewed, (maybe, hopefully) on Thursday at mid-day.

Olympia wasn't fully aware of how much all this group intensity had been getting to her until she started thinking about how good it was going to be to get away from it for a couple of days. Her mother always used to say, "It's like hitting yourself on the head with a hammer. It feels so good when you stop." It was true, she had signed on for the job at

Orchards Cove, but who in the world could have predicted all that had happened once she got there? It was enough to say it had been interesting. If pressed, Olympia would add, "and at times somewhat challenging." It was time for a break and a little personal R & R. She'd more than earned it.

That evening, shortly after supper when Olympia thought she'd settled down in her mosquito-proof screen house with the cats, a glass of wine and a new book, she heard footsteps coming up the path and growled under her breath. She didn't want visitors. She'd been the happy-faced chaplain, meeting and greeting people all day long, and now she was ready for a little solitary confinement. It was Paula and Norris. She sighed under her breath and invited them in.

"We're not bothering you, are we?" asked Norris.

"Not at all, but it will have to be a short visit. I'm dead on my feet, and planning an early night."

"Oh, that's OK, Olympia, we're not staying. We just dropped by to see if you wanted anything from town. We're going to a movie and thought if you needed anything, we could pick it up."

"That's really sweet of you, thank you, but I think I'm good. At least nothing comes immediately to mind."

"OK, then, I guess we'll be going. Did you like the show last night?"

"It was terrific," said Olympia. "How did they manage to get all that done in one week and have it come out sounding so great?"

"Team work and a lot of wiggle room," said Norris. "It damn sure wasn't perfect, not even close, but everybody had fun. That was the main thing."

"Who needs perfect?" said Olympia. It was a rhetorical question.

"See you tomorrow then?" said Paula.

"Tomorrow, yes, but I'm taking off on Tuesday for a couple of days. I'll be back on Thursday. A little R & R for the chaplain while there are so many ministers here. That reminds me. Would you two look in on the cats for me while I'm away? I'd be happy to pay you. I'll leave them inside the tent, just don't let them out. All you need to do is feed and water them. I'll put extra litter in the cat box so you won't have to bother with that."

"You don't have to pay us, Ma'am, we'd be happy to do it. Right, Paula?"

"Absolutely," chirped Paula.

"If you want to hang out here while I'm away, you two could get away from everything for a while, and the cats would love the company."

Norris and Paula looked at each other and said simultaneously, yes, they'd love to, no need to pay them, and thank you, and they'd better get going, or they would be late.

Olympia stood and watched them go, congratulating herself on her quick thinking. It was a perfect arrangement. She had been young once, too.

Twenty-Four

On Tuesday morning Olympia felt like a bird in flight. She was bouncing along, singing with the radio and leaving it all behind her for forty-eight hours and driving north toward Freeport with a song in her heart and her foot on the gas pedal. She had the directions on the seat beside her and two bags of basic groceries, including two bottles of screw-top wine and Jim's beautiful glasses, safely cushioned in the back. Hope springs eternal. You never know who you might meet on a camping trip, right? And you might want to be able to offer him a glass of wine in a proper glass. Of course you would.

The route was pretty straightforward, and in just over an hour the Rev-Doc was turning into the parking area at Pond Side Cabins. Don Blandon, the site manager, welcomed her, gave her a map and a key and told her there was a nightly campfire outside in the circle by the pond and inside the camp shed if it was cold or rainy. Popcorn was free, wine and beer cost two dollars a glass, and coffee, tea and soft drinks were a dollar. On a good night some folks brought musical instruments. Olympia smiled and thanked him. She didn't think there was a brand of wine of a lower quality than what she'd brought with her, but she was willing to be convinced. Either way, she was on vacation, and at two dollars a glass, she'd try anything once. She smiled, thanked him and set off, map in hand, to find her cabin.

The campground was all and more than she'd hoped for. The individual cabins, named after different species of trees, such as oak, maple and birch, were little more than wooden tents with walls, windows and a roof that hopefully kept out the rain, but that's all she was looking for. She was not a pampered-hothouse-flower kind of woman. Indeed, such extravagances made her distinctly uncomfortable. She was a down-to-earth, no-frills person, and this was exactly what she found when she stepped inside cabin No. 5, Tamarack.

She dropped her gear on the floor and looked around at her basic digs. In the one-room structure there were two single beds, both with foam mattresses on plywood bases, a table with two chairs, a floor lamp and an overhead light. Beside the fridge there was a smooth wooden plank workspace with a sink set into it and a two-burner hotplate to the left. The bathroom was a cubicle set into to the back left corner of the structure. It offered a toilet, a sink with a small shelf and mirror above it and a corner shower that looked as if it would spray down the entire bathroom area every time it was used. The Ritz, it wasn't, but funky and charming it its own unadorned way, it most certainly was.

In minutes Olympia was humming a bit of Gilbert and Sullivan and rolling out her sleeping bag. There was a fridge that had to date back to the 1940s, but it was still working. The windows had screens, there was a rocker on the miniscule front porch, and Olympia Brown was in heaven. She had books to read and had even brought her sketchbook and some new pencils along with her. This was not something she got a chance to do very often, but in private moments, when she had the time, Olympia loved to draw. The woods and trees around her and the pond right outside her front door offered her more subject matter than she could ever have wished for.

First on her to-do list was lunch and a nap. Then she might go for a swim or maybe just lie there and read for a while. If she felt like it, she'd check out the evening campfire, but if one more Kingston Trio knock-off started singing "Michael, Row the Boat Ashore," she'd come back to the cabin and drink her own crappy wine all by herself, right out of the bottle.

As it turned out Olympia did not have to drink her own crappy wine in her cabin, and not one single person offered to sing anything by the Kingston Trio. The libation on offer wasn't half bad for a jug wine, and she decided to refill her classy glass a second time. She wouldn't ever serve it to Jim, mind you, but she might try and find a bottle for herself when she went home. Meanwhile, up until then it was as pleasant a way as any to spend a quiet evening. She wasn't looking for excitement. She'd had enough of that over the last several weeks. Nope, this was perfect: the sounds of the pond waters brushing the shore, the wind in the pines and bright stars in a clear sky. Olympia was completely content sitting on one of the logs that served as seats around the welcoming fire, taking it all in.

What did happen that night was, at the point when she was starting to drink her second glass of wine, a soft-spoken man came up and introduced himself as Frederick Watson and asked, in an English accent, if he might join her. Bonus, she thought as she wiggled to the right to make a little more room for him. I'm a sucker for an English accent. I wonder what he's going to turn out to be like?

Don, the grounds manager, now bartender and dispenser of the free popcorn, was also the self-appointed master of ceremonies. When better than half a dozen people were sitting around the fire, he came forward and reintroduced himself and told a short story about how he came to be doing this work. Then he invited each of the campers in turn to introduce themselves say where they were from.

Predictably, some were right at home with this kind of thing and talked easily about who they were and where they called home. Some were more reticent and mumbled their names and hometowns and offered little more. When they'd all had a turn, Don asked them all to go around one more time and briefly tell the group something about the town or city they grew up in. When it came to Olympia, she told them she'd grown up in a big old Victorian house in Hyde Park, which was a sub-section of Boston. The town was small enough so she could walk to school, the shops, her church and the YMCA, where she learned to swim and later would have her first real job as a camp counselor.

"I just came from Hyde Park myself," said the man sitting beside her, the one with the English accent and the adorable twinkle in his eye. Even in the dark, she could see it. "It was just a week ago. I was walking through Hyde Park in London on my way to the train which would take me to Heathrow so I could come here. What a coincidence."

There began the conversation that Olympia and Frederick would continue for a very long time, except neither of them could have possibly known it then. He explained that he was on a self-inflicted first-time visit to the States to do some hiking and by a series of mis-chances had found his way up to Maine and this particular campfire. She said she was on a two-day break from a summer job a bit south of there.

Their conversation flowed easily for the duration of the evening, and when they both began to yawn, he walked Olympia back to her cabin. He left her at the door with nothing more than the casual suggestion that perhaps, if she didn't have other plans, why, maybe they could have a coffee or a spot of tea the next day, but only if she wanted to and she wasn't busy.

"As it turns out, I don't have any specific plans for the day, so yes, I'd enjoy that. Why don't you check in with me before you set off?"

"Right-o, I'll come by and knock you up after I've had my morning cup of tea."

"You'll what??"

"Ooops, sorry about that. English colloquialism, you know. Silly things, really, but one gets used to using them. I'd been warned about these in the guidebook, but I guess I didn't take enough notice. Start again. Miss Brown, may I assume it's Miss?"

"You may." Olympia was trying to stifle the giggles that were on the verge of escaping.

"Miss Brown, may I have the honor of stopping at your door tomorrow morning and inviting you to join me for a cup of tea or coffee or perhaps even breakfast?"

Olympia no longer tried to hide the giggles. "Please do," she said, "and thanks for joining me at the campfire tonight. It made for delightful evening."

"Jolly good," said Frederick, who then turned smartly on his heel and walked away into the darkness.

"Hmm, said Olympia. She was brushing her teeth and addressing the mirror. "Of course I love the accent, but I wonder what he looks like. The light wasn't very good out there. Tomorrow could be interesting!" Then she reminded herself that the man was from England, some three thousand plus miles from where she was standing, and she really must let tomorrow take care of itself.

Twenty-Five

At eight o'clock the next morning, Frederick Watson stood respectfully outside Olympia's cabin door and tapped three times. When she opened the door, he bowed slightly and wished her "Good morrow." She would never tell him she'd been awake and looking out the window since six that morning.

"Why, Frederick, what a surprise."

He looked crestfallen. "But I told you last night, I mean I asked you, if we might spend some time together, and ..."

"Relax. It was a joke, Frederick. I've been looking forward to it, really."

"Oh. That's all right then."

"Let me grab my handbag. I'm assuming you don't have a car, so if you'd like to go find a restaurant, we can take my van."

"Van?"

"I can't wait to introduce you to Van-essa. She's been with me for a long time."

Olympia steered a curious Frederick to the parking area and her beloved faded blue VW van.

"Meet Vanessa. Vanessa, this is Frederick. I'm sure you two will get along. He's from England, and you always were a sucker for an English accent."

After they were seated and buckled in, Olympia turned the key. The old girl rattled into life, and the two went off in search of a traditional American breakfast. They weren't long into the day before Olympia realized she was thoroughly enjoying this man's company, and what a shame it was that he lived so far away. However, she reminded herself, live in the moment. Good advice. Maybe one day she'd even take it.

The two got off to a good start with Frederick having his first ever blue-plate special breakfast at a real 1930s Art Deco American diner. The place was hot, noisy, over-decorated with everything from Rosie the Riveter and Uncle Sam Wants YOU posters to velvet Elvis paintings and thick white coffee mugs. It was a real museum piece of rural Americana. He took a picture of it and then shyly asked if the waitress might take a picture of him and Olympia.

At Olympia's suggestion he ordered the Hungry Man's 2-4-6-8-10 Breakfast and was amazed to discover both sweet and savory foods on the same plate. Two eggs any style, two pancakes with real maple syrup and a great blob of butter melting into everything, two strips of bacon or two sausages, home fried potatoes, toast and, of course, endless coffee.

"Don't you have pancakes and bacon back in England?" asked Olympia. She'd ordered a Mexican omelet with sour cream and salsa.

"Not on the same plate, but I suppose there is a first time for everything, and I am English." He winked and cut into his pancakes.

It only got better from there. By noon they were tentatively and awkwardly holding hands for longer and longer periods of time as they perused bookstores, gift shops and second-hand stores.

The day ended with a sweet kiss, front and center and full on the lips, and a lingering hug before they separated and wished each other a reluctantly chaste good night but not before agreeing to spend the next morning together in search of another American breakfast at another diner. After that, if he wished, she would take him to the bus terminal and send him on his way, and after that she would return to Orchards Cove.

The next morning he was standing at her door at seven, and she greeted him with a more purposeful kiss, which he enthusiastically returned. But reluctant decorum prevailed, and the two set off in search of coffee for the American, tea for the Englishman, and food in abundance for the two of them.

The rest of the morning went far too quickly, and by eleven they were standing beside a rumbling bus, saying their goodbyes. Besides multiple kisses and wistful looks, they exchanged addresses, then wished each other well, and Frederick climbed aboard. She waited on the curb until the bus left, and only then did she turn away.

With a long and heartfelt sigh Olympia climbed back into her van and headed south. It was time to get out of her dreamy little romantic bubble and drive back to the real world, but the happy little bubble refused to be put away and rode right along with her all the way back to her tent in the woods.

When she did get back, it felt as though she'd never left. The cats were pleased to see her. Paula and Norris both welcomed her back and asked if she'd had a nice time. The current conference was in full swing and, according to all, going very well. Olympia's work for the rest of the week was to be on call, if needed, which wasn't very likely with several dozen ministers in residence, and take some time to herself to think about the things she'd planned to do when she took her mini-vacation. In short, what next, Reverend Doctor? You really must pay this some attention.

Also speeding in a southerly direction toward Boston, Frederick Watson adjusted the seat and leaned back in preparation for a few comfortable hours of panoramic window sightseeing. He was charmed by a transport company that would call itself Peter Pan. How American, and how very unlike the home life of our own dear queen, he thought. But to be perfectly honest, his thoughts were not about buses or the British royal family but of the kiss a certain lady minister had planted on his more than willing lips before bidding him adieu and climbing into that disreputable car she insisted on calling Vanessa. He smiled. What a delightful woman she was, and how dull and dreary England would be when he returned.

But England was home, and home is where the heart is, is it not? With a tiny little frisson of surprise, most of all to himself, Frederick realized that might no longer be true. He did have her address in his pocket, and he would most assuredly, write to her. With that settled, Frederick leaned back in his seat and promptly fell asleep.

Twenty-Six

It was past mid-August, and they were in the home stretch. Two more weeks to go before Labor Day weekend, and according to Brad, these were the easiest and most fun of all. The upcoming and second-to-last conference was Gay-Lesbian Trans FIESTA week. This was a high jinks, campy blend of outrageous behavior and desperate courage as a group of people, ravaged by the AIDS epidemic, came together in community and in safety, away from a world that did not often bid them welcome.

"So what exactly will I be doing?" she asked.

Olympia, Brad and Ellie were lingering over coffee on Monday morning.

"Pretty much the usual," said Ellie, pouring herself another half-cup. "These folks are wonderful. They are so appreciative that there would actually be a religious organization somewhere in the world that has made a place for them that they do everything possible to make it easy for us. The only thing I can see is that you might get called upon to do a wedding or two."

"Wedding? People get married up here?" asked Olympia.

Brad nodded. "Indeed they do. Not legally for this group, of course. That day hasn't come yet, but we do ceremonies of holy union all the time. Fiesta Week is really pretty special, you know. Outside of Provincetown in Massachusetts and maybe Fire Island in New York, there are very few places where LGBT people can be out and open and safe together."

I wonder if Spider knew about this, thought Olympia. I wonder if Jim knows about this. Then she answered her own questions: Of course they do. Spider worked here for seven days, and I sent Jim all the literature. Still she couldn't help thinking how wonderful it must be to be surrounded by people like yourself in a religious setting, to be blessed and welcomed instead of shunned and cursed. She shook her head to clear away the internal musings. Brad was speaking to her.

"Huh?"

"They always stage a couple of all-campus events."

"Meaning?"

"On Wednesday there's always a tea dance, on Friday they have the Annual Fiesta Drag Races, and on Saturday night they have a cross-dress senior prom. They call them their fiest-ivities, and everyone is invited—staff, families with kids, crew, the works."

"I'm in. Sounds like fun."

"Oh, it is all of that," said Brad, "and trust me, you'll be exhausted at the end of it. These folks are high energy."

FIESTA Week had thrown Derek completely out of his comfort zone. He had no tolerance for these people, and he never would have. That was one good thing his father had taught him. He straightened his back and steeled himself to be courteous and helpful and nothing more. It was his job to help people, but if one of those fuckers laid a hand on him… Actually, he didn't know what he'd do other than that the very thought sickened him. While he'd never say it out loud, he was glad Spider was gone. Those kinds of people weren't good to have around. Meanwhile, he smiled, kept his head down and his eyes open.

In Portsmouth, New Hampshire, each passing day brought Spider more and more into his own life. Since his first visit with Paula, and there had been two more after that, he'd come out to his parents, was out driving his own car again and making plans to return to Hampshire College in September.

The awful night at Orchards Cove would always be an indelible part of his journey, but even that was fading into perspective as he slowly gained a clearer sense of self and direction. He was still seeing his therapist but had cut the visits back to once a week and had even hooked up with a very low key gay-lesbian group through his local church. To all appearances, everything was coming together.

He smiled as he turned north on I-95. This was the last piece of the plan he'd worked out for himself. It was all part of his ultimate response to what had happened to him that awful day and night back in June. He'd been staying away from home longer and longer now without his parents freaking out. He was proving to them that he was back on track, but they still worried. What the hell, they were his parents. Parents worry. One day they'd learn they didn't need to.

Now he was packed up and off on his own. As far as they knew, he was going up to his grandfather's hunting camp for a few solitary days in the woods. Only he wasn't. His heart beat faster just thinking about what he was going to do. This time he would be in charge.

He drove to the next exit after the one for Orchards Cove and followed the signs to the Rocky Ledge State Park just north of the Cove itself. The park offered hiking trails, scenic picnic spots, seasonal opportunities for birders and a few wilderness campsites with no amenities whatsoever other than a flat place to pitch a tent, a couple of composting toilets and a nearby stream for water and washing up. Before setting off,

Spider went to the nearest everything store and used cash to buy an oversized pup tent and some rudimentary camping gear. He had a flashlight, an all-in-one mess kit and a one-burner butane cooker. Although he'd never camped out in his life, he remembered helping people at the Cove, and remembered pretty much what they had done with this kind of stuff. It didn't look too hard, and it was summer. He'd manage. It's not like he was in a third world country or anything. If he needed something, he'd just go buy it. There were restaurants and convenience stores nearby. It's not like he had to cook if he didn't want to.

The one part of Spider's plan that wasn't completely worked out was the actual face-to-face confrontation with Derek. He knew he could never be free of what had happened that night until he actually confronted him, but exactly how and when that would happen remained a mystery. Because of his earlier explorations, he knew all about the hiking trails and walking paths that interlaced the piney Maine woods between Rocky Ledge State Park and Orchards Cove.

He'd learned that he could come all the way up to edge of the Cove campground without being seen by anyone and that it was half an hour's walk from where he'd pitched his tent. He'd found one spot, a thicket of bushes between the outdoor chapel and the wash house, where he could sit and watch and listen without being seen. He felt like a hunter stalking a deer, but it was more like a spider spinning his web and biding his time. It was exciting, and Spider felt more alive than he had in years. Even if someone did see him, what was one more young man in dark glasses, wearing a hoodie and low-slung shorts, walking along the road or crossing the campground on the way to the wash house?

The scream was unholy and brought everyone within earshot running to Derek's room in the crew shack. As crew boss, he was entitled to have a single and not have to share his privacy with anyone. He was standing beside his bed, nearly as white as the sheet that covered it. On the bottom sheet, near the foot end of the bed, was a dead snake—road kill, no doubt, but now mushy and stinking.

By the time the nearby crew members, dressed in various shapes and styles of sleeping attire, crowded into his room Derek had replaced any trace of white fear with red fury. His thoughts were racing. This was no accident. A rotting snake didn't just get into his bed by itself. Someone, one of them, had put it there. The question was, was this just a sick prank, or did someone actually know of his morbid fear of snakes and put it there on purpose? And if that was the case, who the fuck was it? He immediately ruled out the female staff. This was not a girl thing. By now he was snarling.

"OK, guys, I know one of you did this, and I swear to God I will find out who." He paused and glared at them. "Miguel, get it out of here. I'm not going to do anyone the honor of watching me get rid of it. You're all on alert. I'm not going to say anything to Brad or anyone else, OK? This is between us and it goddamn well better stay that way. Understand?"

The young men and women responded with uncomfortable murmurings.

He looked them over through narrowed eyes and said in a low, tense voice, "The party's over. You can all go back to bed, and pleasant fucking dreams!"

Twenty-Seven

By breakfast time everyone on crew, the entire staff and half the conferees knew every detail of what had happened, and Derek knew they did. He could only hope they took his reaction to finding the snake to be anger, and no one would ever find out what lay underneath that anger.

Brad brought it up at the morning staff check-in, saying that while it was a pretty unpleasant prank, he was convinced it was no more than that, a bit of crew mischief carried, perhaps, to extreme. It was almost predictable as the summer was well past the midpoint, and the tensions of living and working in close quarters were beginning to grow.

"I'll have a talk with the crew this afternoon about the difference between fun pranks and cruel pranks. After that I'll have a private conversation with Derek and see what his thoughts are on the matter. I have to say that while he's done a good job at getting things done up here, we all know I've had to speak to him more than once about being too rigid and demanding. I suppose it's a balancing act. Meanwhile, is there anything else we need to talk about?"

Assistant director Katie Simon waved her hand, and Brad acknowledged her.

"Has anyone else heard any rumblings about petty theft in the campground?"

"What are you talking about?" asked Ellie.

"I can't be sure. You know how these things can grow out of nothing. Maybe it's just collective imagination, but one family reported a missing blanket, and then another said one of their tarps had vanished."

"That's funny," said Olympia. "I had some food go missing a while ago, just a box of crackers and some cheese. I blamed the raccoons and my own carelessness for not securing them."

Brad held up both his hands and shook his head. "Late summer-itis. People are starting to think about going back to jobs and school, and they get preoccupied. Some years it's worse than others. The stuff always turns up. It's either in the trunk of the car, or they loaned it out and forgot. It's a heads up, though. Just because we're almost to the end doesn't mean we can slow down. We have less than two more weeks to go, and for the people who come up here for those two weeks it has to feel fresh and new, even if we are starting to slow down."

Olympia knew exactly what he meant. Life at the college got a little crazy right after finals and before the summer break began. Administration always thought this was a good time to plan staff development programs, and the staff always thought otherwise. Olympia remembered there was usually some academic and personal slippage to be dealt with during this time, but they got through it. No problem, she thought. Been there, done that. It's just a different tee-shirt, that's all.

Only it wasn't. Something was brewing behind the scenes and in back of the crew shed. In the beginning it had just been disgruntled mumblings and mutterings, but now they smelled blood.

Derek Jamison declined the chair Brad offered him, saying he preferred to stand.

Brad shrugged. "Suit yourself. I heard you found a dead snake in your bed last night."

Derek grimaced. "You mean some sick bastard put that snake in my bed. Word travels fast around here, doesn't it?"

Brad nodded unhappily. "Any idea why? I mean, that's a little too gross for a practical joke. You think someone's got it in for you?"

"I can't say I'm going to win any popularity prizes, but that's not why you hired me. I get the work done. According to Nurse Ellie, the place has never looked better. Even after the storm, hell, we were up and running in three days and almost all back by the end of the first week. I even got the chaplain out of the busted-up building without a scratch, remember?"

"I certainly do, and we were all very grateful. But getting the job done isn't everything, Derek, not if it means having a disgruntled or unhappy crew, and this isn't the first time we've had this conversation. For a while you seemed to be doing better. What's happened?"

Derek snapped out of his defiant slouch. "So who's complaining?"

"I wouldn't tell you if I knew, but I don't. General rumblings, like you said yourself, word travels fast." He paused. "Look, Derek, there's no doubt you are doing a good—no, make that a great—job, but you need to lighten up. Word among the crew is that you are still picking on some of them and putting them down."

"Aw, crap. Can't anyone take a joke around here? Everybody ranks on everybody, it's like a game. We all do it. How come all of a sudden I'm the bad guy?"

Brad remained composed as Derek's anger flared. "Maybe you should tell me, or better yet, maybe you should think about what I've just said and see if you can tone down some of your so-called joking. It's clear that some of the crew don't find it funny. Meanwhile, I'm calling a meeting of everyone right after supper to talk about what is and is not an acceptable prank. What they did to you was not acceptable, and they are all going to hear it from me. I'm defending you, Derek, and I will continue to, but you need to meet me halfway. Take it easy on them and yourself. Perfection isn't everything. Good will and compassion count for a lot around here, and whether you think so or not, I'm on your side. I'll see you later."

Derek was wary and on edge as he walked toward the dining hall. He kept to the middle of the road now, nowhere near where anything could jump or slither out at him. The snake prank, if it had been a prank, had totally unnerved him, and he found himself watching everything and everyone for a clue as to who might have done it.

He was also on high alert for real snakes, live ones. He'd been pretty good at assigning himself to jobs where they would be least likely to be: indoor jobs like carpentry, painting and registering guests in the camp office. Even then, every so often he would come upon one, and the cold white fear would engulf him. In quiet moments he allowed himself to question his own sanity in taking a job in a camp if he was so deathly afraid of snakes, but like everything else in Derek's life, he had a reason for doing it. In his own way he was trying to overcome this paralyzing fear, but it wasn't working. If anything, it was getting worse, and his need to conceal it was greater than ever.

That evening in the dining hall, he noted that Paula Budreau and Norris Landrum were sitting together and were now pretty much accepted by all as an item. Derek knew better than to say anything. Still, he found himself grinding his teeth whenever he saw them together. The best he could do was to make sure their work assignments were as far apart as he could make them. Other than that, he was powerless to intervene. He looked over at them, head to head, laughing at some private joke, and turned away in disgust. Were they the ones who had put snake in his bed? Derek had never felt so vulnerable in his life.

The next morning at the regular senior staff check-in, Katie Simon told them all that one of the campground guests reported seeing someone walking alone in the woods out near the chapel.

Brad waved it off. "We get that at least once a year. Somebody reads a creepy novel and scares him or herself into seeing things slinking through the woods. Give me the name, and I'll go down and make reassuring noises. Meanwhile, is there anything else? Everybody OK with how things are going so far? Any problems other than strangers in the woods and people in colorful attire as far as the eye can see?"

There were none to speak of, but Olympia lingered on after the others left.

"Do you have a minute, Brad? It's not exactly a problem, more of a concern. How's Derek doing?"

Brad sat back down in his chair and waved Olympia to another. "Funny you should ask."

"What do you mean?" she asked.

"Something's bothering him. I can see it in his posture and hear it in his voice. He's getting tighter and tighter, if such a thing is possible. I think that snake prank really got to him. Hell, it would get to me too. Somebody up here really doesn't like him, and he doesn't know who it is. That would creep me out. I'd feel like I was being watched every minute."

"Maybe you should speak to him again, see if you can find out what's bothering him."

Brad shook his head. "I just had a talk with him. He needs time to think about what I said. He got off to a bad start, especially with the Spider thing. Not that he had anything to do with it, mind you. At least I don't think so, and I'd have no way of proving it if I did. No, I think he might be coming to terms with the fact that he's made a few mistakes along the way and maybe wishes he hadn't. This place has a way of teaching some pretty profound life lessons, Olympia. Don't ask me how or why, but it does. Maybe it's the whole microcosm thing. You know, everything you need and don't need in your life is right here under your feet, so to speak."

"Maybe so, maybe not" said Olympia.

Twenty-Eight

After leaving Brad's office, and despite what Jim had said about letting Spider make the next move, Olympia went in search of Paula. Most mornings, the housekeeping crew could be found behind brooms and vacuum cleaners, sprucing up the common areas and setting things straight for the guests. She found Paula in the guest lounge outside the dining room.

"Hey, Paula, do you have a couple of minutes?"

"I will shortly. Just let me finish straightening up the books and the board games, and I'll take a break."

"You want a coffee? I'm getting one."

"No, thanks, Olympia, I'll just have some water. Too much caffeine, and I'll be swinging from the trees."

Ten minutes later the two were ensconced in white wooden rocking chairs at the far end of the porch. Olympia got right to the point.

"Have you seen Spider lately?"

Paula shook her head. "Funny you should ask. I was just saying to Norris that I thought he might like to meet Spider, so I called him this morning, and his mom told me he'd gone off for a couple of days by himself. She said he went up to his grandfather's hunting camp. I feel kind of guilty, because since I've been hanging out with Norris I haven't been in touch with Spider very much. Now I'm afraid I'll have to go back and won't be able to see him again. Geez!" She made a little pouty face.

"I'm sure he'd understand," said Olympia. "I was just wondering how he's doing. I suppose he'll be going back to school at the end of the summer."

"Oh, that's for sure. He goes to Hampshire in Western Massachusetts, a very brainy place."

"So I hear," agreed Olympia.

"I'll try calling him again at the end of the week. His mother said it was only for a couple of days. I'll tell him you were asking for him."

"Please do," said Olympia.

That night, long after the lights were out, Spider walked quietly around the Orchards Cove campus. He was learning his way around in the dark, memorizing where things were and who was likely to be seen or see him out there in the wee hours of the morning. He was watching and listening to the rhythms of the place, and he wasn't in a rush. He would have one chance to pull this off and one chance only. Tomorrow night he would take it one step further and slip inside the crew dorm while they were all sleeping.

The next day Olympia found a message in her mailbox to call Jim, and when she did, he said if it was OK with her, he'd like to come up for a couple of days.

"Why wouldn't it be?" she asked.

"Well, you're working, and I don't want to be a bother."

"True, but it's not like I have to hold your hand or anything. That's great. When will you be up?"

"If the hotel has an available room, around suppertime," said Jim.

"And if they don't?"

"I'll find a motel. I'll leave a message and let you know which one."

"Hang on, I'm standing in the office. I'll check right now."

One minute later she was back on the phone with the good news. "There's a room, and I grabbed it for you. Its small and at the back overlooking the parking area, but it's a room, and it's yours. You got lucky. This is a very popular week."

"That's terrific," said Jim, "then I'll see you tonight. I'll come find you after I check in."

Perfect, I'll chill the wine, and I have these two beautiful glasses someone gave me. We can use those."

"No, Olympia, you set out the glasses and I'll bring the wine."

"Deal. See you tonight."

As she walked back to the campground she found herself thinking about how Jim might react to total immersion in something like FIESTA Week. Would it be fun and comfortably familiar or just the opposite?

She was sitting alone and dozing in the late afternoon sun. She had an open book flopped on her chest and both cats curled on her lap when she heard a familiar voice.

"Anybody ready for a glass of perfectly chilled Pinot Grigio?"

Olympia blinked and looked up. "You made good time. I didn't expect you until after five."

"It was a breeze. Midweek there's hardly any traffic. I got out of Boston well before rush hour and zoomed right up here. Now is there a corkscrew anywhere nearby? Don't get up. Just tell me where it is."

She pointed to the picnic table, and Jim, with an uncharacteristic flourish, did the honors. Clearly he was feeling happy, and Olympia was pleased to see it. So often there was a distant sadness in his eyes, but not this afternoon.

He clinked his glass against hers. "Cheers. So tell me what's been happening. Anything exciting?"

"Jim, this is FIESTA week, so every minute is exciting. There's a great lesbian couple camped next door to me." She gestured toward their set-up. "They're nice. I'll introduce you if they get back in time."

"So what's FIESTA like? What do they do all day?"

"It's like any other conference. There are workshops, discussion groups, sports activities, even hymn-sings, the usual stuff. The only difference I notice is that it gets a little outrageous and over the top sometimes, but I think that's probably because it's safe, and they can. There's lots of cross dressing, for example, and no one is going to ridicule or ostracize you for who you are or how you choose to dress. For many, this is the only place they can go where they can really cut loose. It's wonderful, but it's sad, too. It shouldn't have to be that way. It shouldn't have to be a one-week-a-year thing."

Jim looked around. It's a different world, isn't it?"

"I'm glad you came up, Jim. You should experience something like this at least once."

Jim looked thoughtful for a moment before saying, "I hope you're right." Then he brightened. "Say, what about that bully boss you were telling me about last time. Is he any better?"

Olympia giggled. "I probably shouldn't laugh, but somebody pulled a really rotten prank on him last night and put a dead snake in his bed. It totally freaked him out. Turns out he's phobic. We actually had a staff meeting about it earlier today."

"You told me snakes didn't bother anyone up here."

"This was a dead one, road kill probably, and someone put it in Derek's bed. Of course, by the next morning everybody had heard about it, and Derek knew that somebody had it in for him."

"I'd go ballistic too if I found a snake in my bed, alive or dead. I'm terrified of them."

"I didn't know that," said Olympia. "I know you said you didn't like them, but I didn't know it was a big thing."

"Well, it's not exactly something I run around telling people. It's not quite a full-blown phobia but pretty damn close. I wish it weren't."

"It's called ophidiophobia."

"Ophidio-what?"

"Ophidiophobia, fear of snakes. Malcolm and Randall's father was a herpetologist, and before we divorced I spent more than one restless night wondering where the boa constrictor had got to this time. I know a lot about snakes."

"Well, you can keep it all to yourself, Madame. I don't even like to think about them, much less talk about them."

"It's a long shot, but what if Derek is snake-phobic, and someone found out? That would be one hell of a way of getting back at him. Boggles the mind, doesn't it?"

Jim shivered at the thought. "Come on, Reverend, drink up, and let's go have supper. All that driving makes a man hungry."

Olympia held up her glass. "Slow down, Jim. This wine is far too good to toss back. The first bell hasn't even rung yet, and there's still some wine in my glass. You have to learn to savor the moment, you know."

Jim said not a word and simply topped up both of their glasses.

Twenty-Nine

The evening activity was an all-camp talent show, which for FIESTA translated into a high-camp drag show. They had everything imaginable on parade, but most of all they themselves were on display. Olympia counted several Alices in Wonderland and Dorothys on the way to Oz. Also popular were leather strap, zipper and stud outfits which left her wondering how in the world they could sit down in such attire. Finally, a truly Raggedy Ann and Andy with Shirley Temple in tow as their child took the prize for most diversely creative, whatever that meant. Jim just rolled his eyes, and did so on more than one occasion, but it was clear to Olympia that he was enjoying himself.

The costuming and the makeup were so well done that neither Olympia nor Jim was really sure who was spoofing whom, but the result was hilarious. Hilarious with a touch of quiet desperation, thought Olympia as she observed the people around her. Many of the people there for the conference had AIDS or were HIV positive and would likely not be back another time. She knew the look, the dark hollow eyes and sallow blotched skin. It would break anyone's heart, and it tore hers in half. God love them, she whispered under her breath, love them and protect them and let them find joy, even if it is only for a night in a long blond wig or a week at the shore with someone you love.

Although she kept her thoughts to herself, she sensed that Jim might be dealing with his own set of mixed emotions, but she kindly said nothing. When the show was over she walked

Jim back to the hotel porch He gave her a quick hug and said he was exhausted and going straight to bed.

"Must be the salt air," she said with a smile. "You're not tired as much as relaxed, Jim. It's highly beneficial. Go on upstairs and have a good sleep, and I'll see you in the morning."

"Right," said Jim, covering a huge yawn, "and don't talk to any strange skunks, OK?"

Three hours later Spider was standing in the empty hallway outside his old room in the men's dorm. He listened to the unguarded sounds of sleep, the snorts and snuffles, snores and even spoken or shouted words of human beings at their most vulnerable. Some of the doors were standing open to allow the ocean breezes to come through. Others were closed. Very quietly he moved down the wooden corridor, feeling his way along the wall, using the moonlight coming through the window at the end of the space to guide him. He knew exactly where Derek's single room was, last on the left on the ocean side, of course. He got first pick, and he took it.

The door stood slightly ajar. The night before Spider had stood outside that room and listened to the heavy regular breathing and the squeak and creak of the iron camp bed whenever Derek moved. He was a restless sleeper, and Spider was wide awake and hyper-alert as he eased open the door. This was it. Now came the unscripted part.

Jim Sawicki went up the back stairs to his room, but he did not go to bed. He sat on the edge of the bed with his head in his hands. He could hear the sounds of men's voices drifting up from the foyer below him, voices of men laughing and calling out to one another. The voices of men. He reached under the bed, pulled out his suitcase and hastily repacked it. Returning to the front desk, he paid for the one night and signed out. Before leaving, he handed an envelope to the woman on the desk and asked that it be given to Olympia Brown the next morning.

In Derek's bedroom Spider stood motionless at the end of the bed and slipped back the hood on his sweatshirt. Derek, wearing only his underwear, was lying on his stomach. One arm was hanging off the bed, almost touching the floor. The other was wrapped around the pillow and tucked under his head. His mouth was half open, and in the moonlight Spider could see the glint of a thread of spittle on his lips. He was breathing regularly and heavily, totally unaware that his every breath and movement was being carefully and thoughtfully observed.

Spider moved in closer, leaned over the sleeping man and spoke in a low clear voice.

"Derek."

No response.

"Derek!"

Derek's eyes jerked open. "Huh, what? Who ... Jesus, Spider, what the fuck are you doing here?"

Spider grabbed Derek's forearm. "Shut up, and don't scream. I just want to talk to you. If anyone wakes up, I'll tell them we've been meeting here all summer."

"Oh, Jesus, what do you want? Oh, shit no, not that ... not me!"

Spider clamped down harder on Spider's arm. His months in the gym had paid off. His grip was like an iron clamp. "I said shut up. I've got something to say to you, and I've waited all summer to do it. So sit up, I want to look you in the eye."

Derek struggled into a sitting position and pulled the sheet over his lap.

"Oh, for God's sake, man, I am not here for sex, OK?"

Derek nodded, but he didn't relax. Spider pulled up a chair, sat down facing him and began to speak in a low harsh half-whisper.

"Five days after I came up here this summer, I tried to hang myself, but I failed. I tried to kill myself because you humiliated me. You did that by uncovering my secret and threatening to tell everybody up here. At the time I was so ashamed of what I was and so tired of hiding it for all of my life that something in me snapped, and I gave up hope of it ever getting any better. That's when you want to die, Derek, when you lose all hope. And that night, because of what you did to me and what you threatened to do to me, I lost hope."

"I uh …"

"Shut up and hear me out. It's the least you can do, because when I'm finished, I'm out of here, gone like I came in the dark. Unless you say something, no one will ever know."

Derek nodded miserably.

"You're a bully, you know. You're hiding your own fear and weakness by picking on other people. You had it in for me starting on the day I got here, and you never let up. You picked on the other guys, too, and we were all afraid of you, but I was your favorite. You'll have to ask yourself why that was. Did you know I was gay the minute I arrived? Were you curious what it was like? Don't answer that, because I don't care. I tried to kill myself because of what you did to me and how it made me feel. You totally humiliated me. There was more, of course, before I came up here, a whole lifetime of hiding and abuse, but that night you pushed me over the edge."

Derek shifted uncomfortably on the squeaky bed and swiped at his eyes and nose. He was openly weeping.

"You're afraid of something, aren't you, Derek? Most bullies are. You know, I spent a lot of time this summer thinking of how I would get back at you. Then one day I realized I wouldn't know what to do once I did, and so what good was that? That was when I knew what I really needed was to face you down, face the demon and the fear, tell you what you did to me and then walk away from it. In about two minutes that's exactly what I'm going to do but not before I say one more thing to you, and that is, you need to face your own demons, Derek.

"I don't know what they are, and I don't know how they got there. That's for you to figure out. You see, when you try and kill yourself, they send you to the nut-house, and there are some pretty fantastic people there who will help you if you let them. If I hadn't jumped off that dresser I might never have met them, but I did. So I guess in a very weird way, as well as telling you off tonight, maybe I also want to thank you for bringing things to a head."

Spider stood and looked down at the crumpled young man sitting on the bed in front of him. "What you did to me was really cruel, and what did it get you? Look at you, sitting and sniveling in a puddle of your own pee. Yes, I can smell it. You can do better than this, Derek, and I hope to God one day you will."

With that, Spider turned and slipped out of the room as silently as he'd come in.

Derek waited, frozen in place, until he was sure Spider was gone and the dorm was quiet. Before heading for the shower, he stripped off the sheets, balled them up with his underwear and threw it all into the corner. He hadn't wet the bed in years.

Thirty

The next morning there were two letters in Olympia's mailbox. One was a plain envelope with nothing other than her name on the outside. With dismay she recognized Jim's handwriting. The other one, the one she would open when she was alone, was a blue airmail envelope postmarked England, no return address. That one she tucked into her pocket for later and with some trepidation ripped open the one from Jim.

Dear Olympia,
I apologize for my unannounced and hasty departure. Coming here was not a good idea. One day I'll tell you. Bless you for understanding.
Jim

"Oh, dear," said Olympia.

"Bad news?" asked Brad, who had just come in from outside and saw her evident distress.

"Yes and no, maybe. My friend Jim who came up to visit yesterday had to go home."

"Something wrong?"

"That's the maybe part, I don't know. He'll tell me eventually."

"Not something that happened up here, is it?"

Yes and no, thought Olympia.

"I don't think so. He probably got called back to work."

"Really, what does he do?"

"He's a Catholic priest."

"Oh, I see," said Brad.

No, I don't think you really do, thought Olympia, who decided to put off opening the second letter until later on. It was from England, so it had to be from that Englishman she met a couple of weeks ago, Frederick Watson. She patted the letter in her shorts pocket and headed into the dining hall for coffee and food.

Brad caught up with her again just as she was leaving to go back to her site and feed the cats.

"Do you have a couple of minutes? I'm afraid we've got a problem."

"Sure, Brad, what's up? I have to say by the looks of you, it's serious."

"I think it is. Derek just told me he wants to quit, like right now. I'd like you to be there when I try and find out why."

"He might prefer it to be private."

"I think I want a witness."

Olympia's eyebrows went straight up. "It is serious then."

"Derek had a run in with Spider MacCormack last night."

"What? I thought … oh, shit," said Olympia and immediately apologized.

"My sentiments exactly," said Brad. "Derek is waiting for us in my office. I told him I was going to get you. It's for his protection as much as mine. Can you understand that, Olympia? I don't know whether you'll be there as a mediator or a witness or a little of both, but I know we need a third person present."

Olympia nodded and wondered what in earth was coming next, and why in hell they didn't teach a class in employee relations and management when she was at seminary, and where the hell was Spider hiding out?

When Olympia entered Brad's office, she found Derek slumped in a chair. His arrogant, super-sure-of-himself demeanor was gone. He was pale, cracking his knuckles and looking anywhere but at her or Brad. Where and how to begin?

"Hi, Derek. Brad tells me you had a visit from Spider last night. Can you tell us what happened and if that is what has convinced you to leave before the end of the summer?"

Derek shifted again in his chair before clearing his throat and beginning to speak. "Look, I don't know how to say this, but last night I found out I almost killed someone. It wasn't with a gun or a knife or anything, but things I said and did to Spider made him want to kill himself, and he almost did it. If Brad hadn't found him, he'd be dead, and I'd be as good as a murderer. I'm a piece of shit. The crew hates me. Somebody found out I'm wicked scared of snakes and put one in my bed to get back at me. Let's face it, I'm doing a crappy job, and the whole place will be better off without me."

"Do you really think that?" asked Brad.

Derek finally looked up. "You ought to know, you're the director. How many times have we had our little talks? I guess I just don't get it."

Brad folded his arms across his chest and shook his head. "Well, I don't agree with you. You've done a fantastic job of caretaking the place, but you haven't done so well with your crew. You know that, and so do I, but I don't think running away is the answer."

"I'm not running away," he spat, "I'm handing in my resignation. There's a difference."

Brad nodded. "True, and I would rather not accept it, at least for twenty-four hours. That will give you time to think about what happened, why it happened and what, if anything, you can do to make it right. You still have time, Derek. Running won't get you anywhere, but staying and working it through just might."

"I don't see how. I just want to get out of here. I can't face these guys."

"Derek, you were man enough to come and talk to me. You could have just taken off before anyone got up this morning. Legally you still can. I have no hold over you whatsoever. But you stayed. Now stay another day, and think about it. If you need to, take the day off. Go for a walk on the beach or lock yourself in your room, but stay here and think it through."

Olympia, who'd been watching and listening, spoke up. "I know we haven't had much to do with each other, Derek, but I am the chaplain, and if you think it might help, I'd be happy to sit and talk with you. It's up to you, and you don't have to decide now. I'll be down in my campsite all afternoon. It's private there. Just come and find me. We've got some history, remember? On the day of the big storm, you are the one who found me, and you are the one who got me and the cats to safety. That was big. I haven't forgotten that."

Derek shrugged his shoulders. "If you say so. OK, I'll give it twenty-four hours."

"Thank you," said Brad.

By the time she got back to her tent, the cats were complaining, and she was thinking about the number of unhappy men in her life right now: Derek, Spider, Brad and, of course, Jim. She shook her head. Could she do anything to help? Time might or might not tell. She needed a cup of something hot, tea this time, and a quiet hour with the unopened letter sitting in her pocket. There was no return address on the envelope (Now why was that?), but there was no one else in the UK that she knew of who would send her a handwritten letter. It had to be him, Frederick Watkins.

Dear Olympia,
I hope you will not think it presumptuous of me to write, but we did, after all, exchange addresses. I must say I thoroughly enjoyed meeting you two weeks ago in Maine. Since then I have returned to England and set about getting back into my regular routine. Not as interesting as traipsing around the States and meeting lovely ladies in the woods, mind you, but needs must, and I am back to work at the college. Having said all of that, the purpose of this letter is to ask if I might continue writing to you occasionally, as I do so enjoy our conversations. Who knows? We might even meet again sometime.
If your answer is yes, then please write to me at the following address.
Yours faithfully,
Frederick Watson.

"Well, well, well, how very interesting. Maybe there are still a few surprises left for me," said a foolishly grinning Olympia, but her surprise and delight were interrupted by the sound of approaching footsteps. "Damn and blast," she grumbled under her breath. But she had invited Derek to come down and talk to her, and please, God, let me say the right thing, and double please, may it do him some good. She quickly refolded the letter, slipped it back into her pocket and looked up to see not Derek, but Spider MacCormack step into the clearing.

"Spider! Why, uh, what are you doing here?" He looked a little worse for wear, unshaven and rumpled, but otherwise clear-eyed and healthy.

He looked down and flashed her a shy smile. "Hi, Chaplain. I hope you don't mind me sneaking up on you like this, but I really didn't want to be seen by anyone."

Olympia instantly recovered her composure. "Of course. Gee, you look wonderful. Here, sit down. Can I make you a cup of tea? Are you hungry?" It was nervous chatter, and she knew it and took a deep breath. She could do better. She cared about Spider. Slow down, Olympia.

"Come and sit down. Can I get you something?"

He shook his head. "Nothing right now, thanks. I came over here because I wanted to tell you what I did last night unless you've already heard."

"Actually, I have, at least one version. Derek told Brad and me this morning. He was pretty shaken up."

Spider bit his lip and made a face. "That's exactly what I wanted to do, scare and intimidate him. Show him what it feels like. Now I'm thinking maybe it wasn't such a great idea."

"Why is that, Spider?"

He was about to respond but stopped when they both heard the sound of someone else approaching, this time on the main path. Spider leaped out of his chair and slipped behind Olympia's tent only seconds before Derek stepped into view. Oh, my goodness, she thought, never a dull moment in a religious conference center by the sea.

"You said I could ..." Derek was looking acutely uncomfortable.

"Hi, Derek. I'm glad you decided to come. Please do sit down."

He took the offered chair but looked as though he might fly out of it at any moment.

She held up a warning finger. "Before you say anything, let me check on something, OK? I thought I heard a noise behind the tent. I want make sure it's one of the cats and not a raccoon trying to find my food locker."

While this wasn't exactly the truth, it would have to do. Olympia got up out of her own chair and walked around to the back of the tent. Spider was gone, back into the woods as quietly has he'd come. Now what do I do, she asked herself? Keep calm and carry on, her mother would say. Dear, dear mother. Olympia returned to where Derek was sitting.

"Nothing there. I must have been imagining things. Can I make you a cup of tea or something?" Anything to break the tension, she thought.

"No, that's all right. I'm here, but I don't know what to say."

"But you do want to say something."

He nodded.

"Take your time. I'm not going anywhere. This can't be easy for you."

Derek fidgeted and twisted his fingers before finally beginning to speak. "Brad was right, I should stay here and face it, but I don't think I can. I'm not man enough." His voice had dropped to a shaky whisper. "I never have been."

Olympia decided to follow her heart and take a risk. "Who beat you up, Derek?"

The response was instantaneous. "My father." He spoke in a whisper.

"Do you want to tell me about it?"

"Not really, it was pretty awful. He beat up everyone, but me and my mother most of all. He was a drunk, a bad one. He finally killed himself in a car wreck, and believe it or not, I laughed, then I couldn't stop crying. If he'd known, he would have called me a baby. I had to hide that, too. I had to hide that I was scared all the time—scared of him, scared he'd kill my mother, scared of snakes."

"Snakes?"

"Oh, yeah. He used to throw them at me just to watch me go crazy."

Olympia shuddered at the image. "That's inhuman, Derek. It's torture."

He nodded. "I wet the bed until I was fourteen or fifteen, I can't remember now, but it was one more thing for him to beat me up with. I was the wimp son, the one he was ashamed to call his own, so he didn't. He always said my father was the milkman. You can imagine how that made my mother feel."

"He was a monster," said Olympia.

Derek simply nodded and then said, "And I'm turning out to be just like him. Spider had the right idea."

"Derek! What are you talking about?"

"This is no life, not for me or anyone else."

"On the other hand, maybe it is."

Olympia and Derek turned as one to see Spider step out of the woods.

Thirty-One

After a moment of stunned silence, Spider spoke in a kindly voice. "Hi Derek."

At first, Derek looked as though he'd been shot. Then he turned away in shame and stared at the ground. "What are you doing here? Come to finish the job?" he mumbled.

Spider shook his head. "Just the opposite. I think maybe I owe you an apology. I didn't hear everything you said, but I heard enough. What I did to you last night was my way of getting back at you, but what I really did was act just like your father. By sneaking in when you were asleep, I caught you off guard and gave myself the upper hand. Then I made fun of you because you were scared and humiliated. I made sure I had the advantage of surprise, and I made the most of it. Now I see what a rotten thing I did. Two wrongs don't make a right, Derek. I'm being honest when I say I'm really sorry for what I did."

With that, he held out his hand, and after a long moment Derek took it.

Olympia could not believe what she had just witnessed. If she had never believed in miracles before this, she damn sure did now. There was nothing to say other than, "Blessed be, go in peace."

Then she wisely said nothing more and simply let the scent of the pines, the sounds of the birds and the wind in the branches overhead fill the space between them, and it was good.

Finally Derek mumbled something about needing to get back up the hill and left, but not before saying, "Thanks, guys."

Now it was Just Olympia and Spider sitting in the silence.

"Who knew?" said Spider.

Olympia was still at a loss for words but finally added, "If somebody put this in a book nobody would believe it. Talk about life unscripted, Spider, you've just blown me away. That was beautiful. I can't think of any other way to describe it."

"It was the truth, and I guess it saved my bacon, too. Last night after I left Derek's room, my plan was to wait until daylight and get the hell out of here. Then I realized I wanted to see you one more time and thank you in person for staying with me in the ambulance and in the hospital. A lot of what happened that night is still a blur, but I do remember you sitting beside me and talking to me. I was a mess, but you treated me like a human being. I just want you to know it helped."

Olympia could not stop the tears, and she didn't try. "I'm so glad, Spider, and I have to say you look great. Paula told me you were doing well, and just look at you. You really are."

"Paula told you?"

Olympia smiled and nodded. "It must be a great relief to you."

He shrugged. "Yes and no. I am what I am, and it's not a safe place out there for me and my kind yet, but at least my side of the playing field is clear."

"That's a good way of putting it. I like it. The metaphor has many applications. Do you mind if I borrow it for a sermon sometime?"

"I'm honored. Geez, me in a sermon—now that's a switch."

"Not as far away as you think, Spider. My very best friend in the whole world is a gay Catholic priest. He's not as lucky as you are. As long as he's a priest, he can never come out."

Spider grimaced. "Ouch."

Later that day Derek told Brad he would stay on.

Before he left Spider handed a note to Olympia for Paula, saying he was sorry he'd missed her but hoped she and Norris would come down for a visit before the end of the summer. Then he thanked Olympia again for her help and counsel before once more slipping away into the woods, this time on to his new life.

"It's been quite a day," said Olympia, addressing the cats. Two down and one to go. She was very worried about Jim, but for the time being, at least, she knew it was best to stand back and wait for him to reappear, as she knew he would.

Meanwhile, it was back to work as usual at Orchards Cove. These kinds of situations must at all costs be kept from the guests and conferees. They came for rest, relaxation and renewal, and that's what they would get, come hell or high water. Olympia went to bed early that night and slept like the dead.

The next morning, a Thursday, Olympia pulled out her pocket calendar and counted. There were just ten days left of conferences before she could start to pack up. The crew would stay on for a last weekend of clean-up and semi-closing. Then, with the exception of a few three-day, no-frills early fall conferences, all would be battened down and put away for another year. Standing outside her tent, wondering where to start and how in hell she was going to get it all into one vehicle, Olympia was ready to go home.

Ten more days. Please, God, no more crises, not of nature, not of the spirit, not of the heart. It had been an eventful summer, and while she was glad she'd come up and felt she had more or less accomplished what she'd set out to do, she was mentally finished and ready to go home.

She had met a couple of men and had a couple of dates. Interesting, but not worth telling her mother. On the other hand, there was that Frederick Watson person. He had potential, or rather he would have if he didn't live on the other side of the Atlantic Ocean. Ah, well, at least I'm a fifty-year-old with a new pen pal. How quaint! I'm hungry. It must be time for breakfast.

The last few days did fly by, and they were uneventful. For that they all were profoundly grateful.

Derek did stay on, and in those last ten days he was a very different man. The rest of the crew never knew what had happened that night, but they all knew something had and seemed to breathe a bit easier because of it. Still, they wondered, and for once there was no gossip to explain the change.

Sitting together and enjoying their last breakfast together, Ellie and Olympia promised to keep in touch, but when asked if she would be back the following summer, Olympia smiled and shook her head.

"This was a one-off, Ellie. I'm glad I did it, but once was enough. I did learn that I will probably go more in the direction of more traditional ministry and chaplaincy in the future, but that depends on whether or not I sell the house."

"You putting your house up for sale?" asked Ellie.

"I am. Instead of reading the personal ads, I started picking up the Boston papers and reading the real estate ads. This seems like a good time to sell. That's another reason I need to get right back. I have about ten days before I have to start teaching, and there's a lot of running around to do before I actually put it on the market."

"Do you know where you're going to move?"

Olympia shook her head. "Not exactly. Part of me wants to get a low maintenance condo in the city and be closer to work. But I may or may not stay on at the college too much longer, so the other part of me would like to get an old fixer-upper with a ton of character and see what happens."

"That takes courage, especially being single." Ellie looked at Olympia over her coffee mug.

"Courage or dumb-assed stupidity," laughed Olympia. "When I decide which, I'll let you know."

Ellie grinned and shook her head. "You are certainly a character, Madame Reverend! I'm so glad we've met. Whatever happens, please keep in touch, OK?"

"Oh, yeah. You're a keeper."

At three in the afternoon Olympia was standing, hands on hips, dirty and sweat-streaked, in the empty space that had been her home base for almost ten weeks. She'd done it. Somehow she managed to get tent, chairs, dining canopy, Jim's lovely wineglasses and both cats back into the van. Standing there listening to the sound of the wind in the trees and the distant roar of the ocean that had been her ambient background music all this time, she felt curiously sad. As eager as she was to be on the road and back home and sleeping in her own bed, she also felt a sense of loss. This had been a once-in-a-lifetime summer. She'd already declined the invitation to return, and now she was moving on, but to what and away from what?

She'd accomplished what she'd set out to do in coming to Orchards Cove. She'd given serious consideration to what she planned to do with the second half of her life and was reasonably satisfied with the outlook. She would stay on at Merriwether for at least another year, possibly two. She would seriously think about selling her house, but where might she go? That remained a question mark, but it no longer was a source of concern. If she got a good offer on her present house, she'd move, and if she didn't, she'd stay put, at least for the time being.

On the more personal front, she'd had two real dates—well, three if she counted the day with Frederick Watson, and while it hadn't exactly been a social whirlwind, at least the breezes were stirring. She'd sent Frederick a prompt response to his first letter with her home address and the clear invitation to send his next letter there.

Now what? Her last official Orchards Cove act was to have a long, hot shower, say her final goodbyes and get on the road. She picked up the fresh clothes she'd left out, the remaining sliver of soap, a ratty looking towel and the last of her shampoo and headed to the wash house. There she stripped off her clothes and gleefully, piece by piece, threw them into the wastebasket. When she finished her shower and was dressed in clean clothes, she threw in the towel, as well. She thought about the symbolism of the metaphor she'd unconsciously created, but didn't dwell on it for long. She had miles to go before she slept. It was time to go.

Thirty-Two

On a warm evening in late September, The Reverend Doctor and still college professor Olympia Brown and Father Jim Sawicki were pretty much back to business as usual. She was teaching Humanities and Religion at Merriwether and doing some occasional preaching in local churches. He was teaching at Allston College full time and serving in the neighborhood parish of St. Bartholomew's in Dorchester. By some holy mystery, they found they had the same unscheduled afternoon, and Olympia took advantage of same to invite him to come to dinner and check out the historic fixer-upper house she'd recently purchased and was already moved into.

Jim hesitated. "So you did buy it."

"Jim, I couldn't not. They seriously dropped the price on the same day I got a cash offer for the Edgewater house. I told you I was ready for a change, so why not start where I live? I can't wait for you to come and see it.

"Uh, just how much of a handyman special is this thing? Do I bring hazard gear, a hammer, a paint brush or a bulldozer?"

She laughed. "All of the above, my friend, but not tonight. Bring some wine, and we'll get take out. The kitchen isn't fully workable yet, and I keep losing the cats in the rubble, but they're making short work of the mice that came with the place, which means I'm saving on cat food, too."

This produced a hearty chuckle on the other end of the line. "Are you sure you shouldn't camp out in a motel or something until it's habitable?"

"Hell, no. It's not cold yet, and I have hot water and a toilet that flushes. The doors and most of the windows work. It just needs a major clear out, and I'm working on that. It's been empty for about five years, and the person who lived here before that never threw anything out. It's not dirty, just major clutter and crap everywhere. The good news is, I made enough on the sale of the old house that I can get started fixing it up right away."

"What do your sons think about your selling their childhood home?

"Oh, they wailed a bit, but they really are pretty much out on their own now. Malcolm is living in Somerville, and Randall is finishing up at UMass Amherst. They will have rooms here, if they need them."

"Look, why don't we finish this conversation face to face? Do you have any furniture yet, or do I bring my own orange crate?"

"Funny you should ask. Most of my stuff is still in storage. I'm sort of camping out in the great room off the kitchen. I do have a table, two chairs, a working stove and a fridge. I'm good."

"So where is it?"

"Would you believe I'm still in Brookfield? So much for moving into the city. This place is not even two miles from the other one. It's in the old section of town. Many of the houses here go all the way back to the 1700s."

Jim groaned. "Does yours?"

"Seventeen thirty-nine. I plan to research it later on, maybe even in another lifetime."

Olympia gave him the address and clear directions, then looked around in mild dismay at the heaps and piles of stuff that were going to be the setting for her first official visitor. She did have two chairs, the aluminum camp chairs she bought after the storm from hell that summer, plus a card table that didn't wobble as long as she put a matchbook under one of the legs. All this and a working telephone was everything she needed for now. Maybe someday she'd have someone to share it with. She shook her head. Nope, first things first, like a roof over my head that doesn't leak.

Jim arrived exactly on time and was courteously reserved in his praise of Olympia's new digs. She was right, it was a fixer-upper (and then some), but she was also right in that it had real character. In fact, if he were to describe it even from his first visit, he'd say the house had a distinct personality, and if the house could respond, it would have told them it was tickled pink to have occupants once again. It would go on to say that it had been far a too long stretch of emptiness, and so now, let the merriment begin.

But houses can't talk, and thus it remained silent. Still, this house would have no end of mysteries and surprises for Olympia and her soon-to-be extended family in the weeks and years ahead. Therein lies a tale –several, actually. More anon.

"What shall we order for dinner? Within five minutes' driving distance of this kitchen we have Chinese, Thai, pizza and a fish place."

"Have you tried the fish?"

"No, you know I'm vegetarian, but I hear tell it's great. Very popular. Why don't we get fish for you, and I'll get Thai? The two places are only minutes apart."

Jim looked crestfallen.

"What's the matter?"

"Oh, dear, I may have brought the wrong wine."

Olympia rolled her eyes. "Give me the phone."

Later, sitting on the aluminum chairs, the table cleared of the take-out and steaming cups of Irish coffee between them, the two friends settled in for the evening. They'd decided by the end of the second glass of wine that Jim should not drive and would stay the night. Olympia was sure somewhere in all of this they could find something that would do for a bed, but looking at the monumental clutter surrounding them, Jim wasn't so certain.

As is so often the case when two friends have a couple of glasses of wine and the hour grows late, the words flow more easily. Slowly their conversation meandered from ideas for her new old house to possible future career plans and ideas. Finally Jim asked her about the past summer and her Orchard Cove experience.

She gave him a thoughtful look. "We haven't really had a chance to talk since I got back, have we? What with starting up my classes and buying, selling and moving house, I really haven't had an opportunity to process it all." She paused. "The short answer is, all in all, I think it was good. It turned out to be way more intense that I expected, more than anyone could have expected, I think, but I'm glad I did it. I wanted a change, and I damn sure got one. I think I did some good up there, as well."

"You mean with that poor kid who tried to hang himself? I have to say, that was a terrible first day for you—for anyone really."

Olympia nodded. "I guess I haven't told you, have I? Come to think of it, we've barely had five minutes on the phone since the night you left the Cove."

Jim made a face. "Sorry about that."

"Sorry about what?"

"Just up and belting out of there like that without a word of explanation. I mean, I probably could have done better than just leaving a note in your mailbox. That was rude."

Olympia reached out and put her hand over Jim's. "I figured something happened to unsettle you, and one day you might tell me. Then again, you might not. Either way, my mother always used to say, don't bother with excuses. Your friends don't need them, and your enemies don't believe them."

Jim half chuckled. "True. You know, I really would like to meet this famous philosophical mother of yours one day."

"Don't hold your breath."

"Why do you say that, Olympia?"

"Mommy dearest is not all that fond of Catholics in general and distrusts any and all clergy."

"But you're a minister yourself."

"Right in one," said Olympia. "It positively made her day when I made that decision. But let's go back to the Cove. There is a happy ending for the young man who tried to take his life. He came back to see me before the end of the summer. He's doing well. As a matter of fact there were several happy endings up there. I just wish yours was one of them."

"Taking off in the middle of the night wasn't a bad ending for me, Olympia. It was a bad decision to go up there during FIESTA week. At first I thought it would be a time out of time when I wouldn't have to be so guarded, but I was wrong. What I found was too much of what I gave up and can't have all swirling around me. You know, look but don't touch. I knew I had to get out of there before anything happened. Too many memories, too many temptations."

He looked away and began rubbing his chin.

"I'm sorry," she whispered.

"Me, too," said Jim, "but I got back, and I got over it. One does. God bless the sacrament of reconciliation, formerly called confession. Anyway, I'm clean and wiser for it. You started to tell me about that young man, Alligator or something."

Olympia laughed. "Close, it's Spider. Anyway, it took him the whole summer, but he found a way to come back and face down his tormentor and come out on top. It was really amazing."

"Before you say any more, how about a little more of that special coffee you made us?"

"Sounds like a plan," said Olympia. "You want some more whipped cream on it, too?"

"Is the Pope a Catholic?"

She made a face. "Jim, I know the Pope's a Catholic, but does he like whipped cream?"

The next morning, both Jim and Olympia were slow to get moving. But hot strong coffee and a good breakfast—she did have bread, butter, milk and eggs and a working stove—soon put the two of them right and ready to face the day. Whether it was priestly decorum or some vestigial scrap of modesty, Jim had elected to sleep outside the house in Olympia's van. She'd slept in it more than once and knew the back seat pulled out into a cozy and most comfortable queen-sized bed.

"Were you comfortable enough out there?" she asked, still rubbing the sleep out of her eyes.

"I probably could have slept in the bathtub and not noticed it, I was so tired, but who knew you'd still have a sleeping bag and a pillow in your van. All I needed was a teddy bear."

"I don't clean out my van very often, Jim, and see, it was a good thing I didn't. I never know what I might need when I'm out on the road."

Jim just shook his head. There was no response for this. He poured them each a fresh cup of coffee instead.

"OK, we got our past lives sorted out last night, so what about the future? You first, Olympia."

She leaned back in her chair, stretched out her legs and settled in for the long haul. Good thing it was a Saturday. Good thing she was with her best friend. Merriwether, papers that needed grading and all that went with it could damn well wait. She blew on her coffee, took a sip and began.

"This house will likely be a big part of whatever is my future. It's going to keep me off the streets for some time. It's livable, but it needs work—a lot of work. You know I like to have a project. Well, this is at least fifty projects all under one roof."

"How much do you know about house repair?"

"Enough. I can paint and plaster walls, do some minor carpentry and make telephone calls when I can't. I'm in no rush. It's not like I have a galloping social life or anything close to it to distract me, so I might as well work on my house."

"You do like rescuing things, don't you? Old houses, stray cats, orphaned priests, what else? Make sure you call me when you need a hand. Believe it or not, underneath this elegant exterior beats the heart of a handyman."

"Fooled me," said Olympia.

"I am the second son of a west-end-of-Boston Polish housepainter. I used to help him out when I was a teenager. I can wield a paint brush and a hammer with the best of them. I actually enjoy getting my hands dirty once in a while."

"You're kidding. You may be sorry you told me."

Jim leaned back and finished his coffee. "I don't think so, and now, changing the subject with no advance warning, what about Merriwether? I take it you're going to stay on there at least for the foreseeable future." He paused and cocked his head. "Say, did you just hear something? Is there a clock in here somewhere?"

Olympia frowned. "Not that I know of. I have a little travel alarm, but that's over there by the sink. What did you hear?"

"I could swear I heard a clock chime. You didn't hear it? It sounded like it was in the next room." He pointed to the great room off to his right.

She shook her head. "I just told you I didn't, but it wouldn't surprise me. This place is full of odd sounds, creaks and groans and grunts and such. Along with the clutter and the old furniture, there's almost two hundred and fifty years of collected human history, aka junk, in this place. It's probably a ghost, or maybe even two, or a ghost that likes to keep time. The place is old enough."

"You're joking, of course." Jim arched an eyebrow in her direction.

"Actually, I'm not. According to the locals, many of the old houses around here have, uh, spirited inhabitants. They all seem to get along. I'm sure I'll find out one way or another soon enough."

Olympia stood up and began collecting the cups and spoons. "I can't afford to stop working at the college with a new house under my wing. I'll be good for a while longer at least. Teaching is getting old, though. The kids are great; they always will be. Its politics and the shifting academic sands that are getting to me. You know, one year collaborative learning is the best thing since sliced bread, then everyone has got to learn how to use computers." She rolled her eyes. "That'll be the day."

Jim pointed his index finger at his friend. "The day has come, Olympia. Allston installed them in all of our offices over the summer. It's sink or swim time."

She sighed. "I suppose, but I'm going to put it off as long as I can."

"Remember what people said about automobiles? They were supposed to be a passing fad, too."

"This is different. Computers are weird. I don't trust them."

"Luddite!"

"And proud of it."

Olympia hesitated and got a funny look on her face before continuing. "Then there's Frederick. I should probably tell you about him."

"Frederick? So you did meet someone through the personal ads after all?"

She shook her head. "No, that turned out to be an exercise in futility. All wind and no rain, so to speak, but after that storm last summer, I probably shouldn't make such jokes."

"Olympia, you're stalling. Who is Frederick?"

She smiled and looked off to the side, evading his direct stare. "Oh, just somebody I met in Maine. He's English. We've been writing back and forth."

"Are you going to tell me anymore about him?"

She smiled and shook her head. "Not until there's something to tell. The man lives in England, and I live here. He's very sweet and unfortunately very geographically inconvenient. Just my luck. He's a great conversationalist though."

Jim wisely said nothing more on the subject.

"So new house, lots of projects, you're staying on at the college, and you've got yourself an English pen pal. Have we left out anything?"

Olympia stopped wiping off the table top and looked at her friend.

"There is one more thing, Jim, I want to find my daughter."

Preview A Deadly Mission, the first Olympia Brown Mystery, at the end of this book.

Meet Author Judith Campbell

(Rev. Dr.) Judith Campbell is a Unitarian Universalist Community Minister. In addition to the Olympia Brown Mission Mysteries, she writes poetry, short stories, children's books, and articles on religious faith and the creative spirit. She offers writing workshops and retreats across the US and annually in the UK. She lives with her husband, Chris Stokes, and two thoroughly spoiled felines in Plymouth, Massachusetts, and on Martha's Vineyard. Rev. Judy loves to talk with readers and answers every e-mail personally. She is available to preach in your church and/or lead a retreat or workshop, or speak in your local library or bookstore. Just say when! Visit Judy at www.judithcampbell-holymysteries.com. Put your name on her mailing list, and get all the latest news on the comings and goings of Olympia Brown and friends.

~

Frequently Asked Questions

FAQ: Is there a strong element of memoir/autobiography in your books, and in the character of Olympia?
ANS: Oh, yeah!

FAQ: Do you plot out your books before you sit down to write them?

ANS: No. I start with a theme. In *A Twisted Mission*, it's bullying. Then I line up my characters in my chosen setting, in this case a church conference center, and turn them loose. The location or setting always figures into the story as do the personalities of the characters. Like so many authors, I often have the experience of a totally unexpected/unplanned character just walking in and making her/himself a vital part of the story. I love it when that happens. I like being surprised as much as I think my readers do.

FAQ: What drives your protagonist? What is her underlying issue that makes her do what she does?
ANS: Good question, and one agents and reviewers often ask. Olympia is perennially trying to save and protect the marginalized and the underdog. When I first began the series, she originally had a gay younger brother who committed suicide, and because she feels she failed him, she spends the rest of her life trying to help others in need or personal crisis. That need to help others remains the same, but I changed the younger brother into a child she had out of wedlock and gave up when she was seventeen. It's a much stronger element, and the search for that daughter has become one of the main subplots of the series.

FAQ: Did you have a daughter that you gave up?
ANS: I did not, but throughout my life and more lately in my ministry, I have known so many people who have either lost children or found them or been found by them, I feel I can speak to the issue with compassion and authority.

FAQ: So you really are a minister?
ANS. Yes, I really am.

FAQ: Who are your favorite authors?
ANS: Elizabeth George, Ann Perry, Donna Leon, Tony Hillerman, John D. MacDonald, PD James (God rest her creative soul.), Elizabeth Berg, Ann Tyler, Anne Lamott, Bill Bryson, Donna Tartt, and of course, moi-meme! I love my own books. That's why I write them.

FAQ: Anything you want to add to this?
ANS: Yes! Do please write to me, revdocmom@comcast.net. I really do love talking to my readers. Ask me more questions. Challenge me with a story idea. More than one friend has done that, and I've actually used them in my books. Finally, word of mouth is the best advertisement. If you like my stories, tell your friends, ask your local bookstore and library to carry them, give them as gifts, and pass them on. My writing is part of my ministry. It is how I feel I can make people aware of some of the injustices in the world and what they might be able to do to make it better. No, they are not preachy. I promise you that. They are good stories that I believe need to be written, and I am doing it. Thank you—and bless you for picking up and reading this book.

Further Thoughts

Because there is often a social or moral issue that is part of my work, when I can, I like to offer sources of further information for those of you who might need it for yourself or know someone who does. In this case, I offer some websites for LGBT (Gay, Lesbian, Bisexual and Transgender) issues:

http://community.pflag.org
(Parents and Friends of Lesbians and Gays)

US Government websites on LGBT issues:
http://www.itgetsbetter.org
http://www.cdc.gov/lgbthealth/youth.htm
http://www.glaad.org/

And for people who want to know more about or need help in dealing with bullying:
http://www.stopbullying.gov/
http://www.pacer.org/bullying/resources/info-facts.asp

Preview of the <u>original</u> first title in the Olympia Brown Mystery Series, also from Mainly Murder Press

A Deadly Mission
by Judith Campbell

One

The trash collectors knew better than to touch the body of the young woman they found sprawled in the alleyway behind the flower shop. While the younger of the two ran off to get help, the older man stayed, trying not to stare at the emaciated figure lying at his feet. The thick, sweet scent of rotting leaves and broken flowers spilling out of the trash container beside them smelled like death, like his mother's funeral.

From where he was standing, the man with a teenage daughter of his own could see a white plastic band around the dead girl's wrist and the glint of something shiny in her hand. Her only article of clothing was a hospital johnny tied in a ragged bow at the back of her neck.

Later that day, the Medical Examiner for the City of Cambridge would pry a silver cross engraved with the words *Jesus loves you* out of her cold, stiff fingers.

Two

Brother David was pacing, circling the room like a wolf stalking its prey. Despite the early summer heat, the windows in the upstairs room were closed, and only a small fan, grinding away in the corner, did anything to move the humid air around the people at the table.

David was an intense, restless man with the thin, muscular body of a distance runner.

"The answer to your question, Brother Aaron, and any other question you might have, is always going to be here."

He held up an open Bible and began reading aloud, stabbing at the page with his index finger and punctuating the words with the squeak of his sandals on the polished oak floor.

"For this cause a man shall leave his father and his mother, and shall cleave to his wife; and they shall become one flesh. And the man and his wife were both naked and were not ashamed."

He paused and looked at the four people seated around the table. Spittle was collecting at the corners of his mouth.

"Everything we know and live by is in this book. We are called to leave the material world and enter into this fellowship of believers so we may follow in the footsteps of Jeshua ben Josephus and like him, do the work of His Abba, Yahweh. The Bible tells us that when the time comes for a man to have a wife, a wife will be made available to him."

"And it came to pass, when men began to multiply on the face of the earth, and daughters were born unto them, that the sons of God saw the daughters of men that they were fair; and they took them wives of all which they chose. Genesis six, verses one and two," said Aaron looking up at the wiry man who was now standing over him. Aaron cleared his throat.

"But if some of us, uh, feel we might be ready to have wives, shouldn't we be able to say something?" The seated man looked down and began picking at one of his fingernails.

"For us, this means ..." said David, ignoring the question and glancing briefly at the woman sitting away from the others near the end of the table. "This means that when the time is right for a man to have a wife, the Abba of this Christian Fellowship will provide one."

Aaron nodded but said nothing. It was best to go along with David when he got like this. Sister Miriam and Brother Joshua, sitting opposite Aaron, exchanged a quick look but remained silent.

"Our Abba is wise, Brother Aaron. You need to trust him." David moved nearer the window, his voice returning to a more conversational level. "There's one more thing. Before we adjourn, we need to set a time to review our new member policies." He hesitated and cleared his throat. "As you know, earlier this year, we had an aspirant who became too zealous in her preparation. Her death was an accident, of course, but such things could reflect badly on us."

David closed the Bible and began walking toward the woman who had seated herself a little apart from the others.

"Meanwhile, Sister Sarah, have you made all the arrangements for the summer Praise and Glory Concerts on Boston Common? Permits? Newspaper advertising? Campus posters?" He paused. "Anything I might not have thought of?" He emphasized the personal pronoun.

Like the other woman in the room, Sister Sarah was dressed in loose-fitting, modest attire. As David approached, she tucked a dark wisp of hair under her headscarf.

"You've covered everything, Brother David." She turned and looked at the man now standing next to her. "Am I right in assuming we won't be doing the Bible study groups until the fall, unless, of course, you want to try running them in the summer? They've been effective."

"Thank you, Sister. We've found the concerts work best for the summer population. The other is more labor intensive and better suited to the traditional academic cycle, but you're always thinking, aren't you?"

Sarah shifted in her chair, edging away from the electric heat of the man. She began tracing a long, thin scratch on the surface of the table with her fingertips.

"Thank you, Brother David, but may I be excused? I think the heat is getting to me."

Three

Professor of Religion Olympia Brown and her longtime friend, Father Jim Sawicki, had just returned from their end-of-semester lunch date. She had been rattling on about her expanding plans for the tumbledown antique farmhouse she'd recently purchased, while he, the ever-prudent Jim, suggested she consider doing some of the more necessary repairs before actually taking up residence. Olympia was explaining how she couldn't afford to maintain two houses when she saw the white envelope taped to her office door.

After unlocking the door and offering Jim a seat, she heaved open a resistant window to let in some air.

"So we both know what I'll be doing this summer," she said, settling into her own chair and ripping open the envelope. "I'll be digging through two hundred years of accumulated … Jesus, Jim, listen to this."

Her hands began shaking as she read the contents of the letter aloud.

> *To members of the Merriwether College Community,*
>
> *We regret to inform you that on May twenty-seventh of this year, first-year student Sonya Wilson died as the result of a tragic accident. At the request of her family, funeral services were private. The college plans to honor her memory at this year's commencement ceremony.*

Donations may be sent to the Sonya Wilson Memorial Scholarship Fund, established by her parents and the College Board of Overseers.

"This is such a goddamned whitewash," said the Reverend Doctor Brown, mashing the letter into a crumpled wad and flinging it across the room.

"Really, Professor!" Jim leaned back and arched a well-groomed eyebrow.

"Oh, shut up, Jim." Olympia started to raise her hands but then dropped them back on her lap. "I'm sorry, but it's not funny. This is the official word on that freshman they found dead last week, Sonya Wilson. I told you about it."

Jim nodded.

Olympia ran her hand through her short, salt-and-pepper hair. Anything further about the possibilities and eccentricities of her new old house would have to wait until another time.

"The whole thing started last January. Sonya started hanging out with a religious group called The Boston Christian Common Fellowship. By February break she was losing weight, a lot of weight. I tried talking to her, but all she would say was that it was Jesus' will, and The Fellowship was watching over her."

Jim started to say something, but Olympia ignored him and kept on with her story.

"I called the Dean, but he said students go on crash diets all the time, and unless it was a life-threatening situation, confidentiality policies forbade his contacting a student's family."

Olympia blew out a long breath in exasperation and pushed at the perennial clutter of papers on the desk in front of her.

"When I approached him a second time, he actually called me into his office and told me that my job was teaching and providing spiritual support for the students and nothing more. He said that if I went ahead on my own and contacted her parents, there could be, as he put it, consequences. He's got a power thing with me, Jim, but that's another story."

Jim listened. His time would come.

"I had no idea it was so bad. I should have done more to try and help her."

"I'm not so sure you could have," said Jim. "Religious fanatics are just that, fanatic, without reason, unreachable. So are anorexics, for that matter, if she was, in fact, anorexic."

Olympia tried to steady her voice. "The day before she died, she got so weak she passed out and landed in the hospital, but she managed to sneak out during the night. The next morning, her body was found behind a flower shop outside Harvard Square."

Olympia took off her oversized glasses, held them up to the light, made a face, and began polishing them with the edge of her blouse.

"I never told the Dean, but I actually went down to Cambridge Police Headquarters myself and asked to see the report." She shook her head. "The official cause of death is listed as complications due to anorexia nervosa."

Olympia shook her head and looked at her friend. "But that's not the whole story, and the administration isn't talking. Nobody wants to deal with what led up to it and ask how such a thing could have happened at lily-white, upper-middle-class Merriwether College."

Olympia was pouring out a semester's worth of anger and helpless frustration to the one man in the world she trusted, an intensely private, drop-dead handsome, gay Catholic priest.

The two met years earlier at Harvard Divinity School a few blocks away from where they were sitting. He was the student chaplain at nearby Allston College, and she was a professor of humanities and chaplain at Merriwether, a small women's college located in a pricey residential section of Cambridge, Massachusetts.

What began as casual conversations about their respective jobs slowly evolved into a deep and trusting friendship. Two late-career clerics with widely divergent theologies discovered they shared a profound commitment to making a difference in the lives of the people they served despite the consequences. They also shared a penchant for challenging the religious and academic establishment.

She was a mid-life and round-in-the-middle remnant of the sixties whose casual dress and easy manner belied a sharp intelligence and a ready wit. By contrast, he was much taller, more conservative in both personality and style of dress, and inclined to periods of quiet introspection.

The priest looked at his friend, knowing what was coming next, but courtesy and habit decreed that he ask.

"What are you going to do?"

Olympia straightened up in her chair. "I'm convinced her weight loss and death are related to that Fellowship group. I want to know what it was these people said or did that killed her."

Paperback or e-book for Kindle versions at Amazon.com
E-book versions for other reading devices available at Untreedreads.com

CPSIA information can be obtained
at www.ICGtesting.com
Printed in the USA
FFOW02n2117140415
12613FF